"What are y

Sara's tone was puzzled as Darius pulled up in front of a lodge. This wasn't a scheduled stop.

"Getting us a room." He turned off the ignition and smiled at her. At last. He'd been going crazy for the last hundred miles, thinking of his surprise.

As she looked into his eyes, her heart swelled with love for this sensitive, sexy man. "But—"

Leaning over, he pressed a quick, hard kiss against her lips. "Humor me," he said quietly. "I want to sleep with you in a real bed. A wide, soft one, with fat, fluffy pillows and a down comforter."

She sighed in happiness. Each night with him had brought pleasures she'd never imagined, even in her most romantic fantasies. It seemed as though tonight would bring more. "Darius, I do like your style."

He clasped her left hand between his and squeezed. "Believe me, you haven't seen anything yet."

JoAnn Ross never seems to run out of ideas. For Temptation alone she has now written thirteen books in four years, each one fresh, lively. . . and very sexy. *Wilde 'n' Wonderful* is no exception, and this moving romance lives up to its title. JoAnn credits her constant stream of new ideas to her fertile imagination and her sometimes childlike ability to see adventure and magic everywhere. "I go through life pretending to be a grown-up, and I manage to fool most people."

Books by JoAnn Ross

HARLEQUIN TEMPTATION

115–A HERO AT HEART
126–MAGIC IN THE NIGHT
137–PLAYING FOR KEEPS
153–TEMPTING FATE
171–HOT ON THE TRAIL
187–WORTH WAITING FOR
193–SPIRIT OF LOVE
201–IN A CLASS BY HIMSELF

HARLEQUIN INTRIGUE

27–RISKY PLEASURE
36–BAIT AND SWITCH

Wilde 'n' Wonderful

JoANN ROSS

Harlequin Books

TORONTO • NEW YORK • LONDON
AMSTERDAM • PARIS • SYDNEY • HAMBURG
STOCKHOLM • ATHENS • TOKYO • MILAN

To Mabel Atkins,
who reads every book and
always says such nice things

Published July 1988

ISBN 0-373-25309-5

"I SIMPLY CANNOT believe that you, of all people, are doing this to me!"

Sara McBride's distressed expression was at odds with the subdued, elegant ambience of the Barclay Hotel dining room in Philadelphia. White-and-green brocade was reflected in the mirrored pilasters. Finger bowls filled with fragrant water rested beside each Lennox place setting while a waiter in black tie hovered nearby, anxious to please.

The curry tray—two curries with an assortment of condiments—was undoubtedly delicious, but Sara's mind was not on the excellent lunch, nor the attractive surroundings. She was staring at the woman she had, until now, considered her best friend.

"Really, Sara," the impeccably groomed woman across the table complained, "you are simply not looking at the big picture."

"The big picture."

Germaine Wingate nodded as she fitted a cigarette into a slender ivory holder. There had been a time, forty years ago, when Germaine was the most popular fashion model on the continent. She'd been wined and dined by politicians and princes, sultans and film stars. When she was nineteen, there was a rumor making the rounds that she was secretly married to Howard Hughes; when that proved false, another story leaked out, alleging that she had eloped with the Aly Khan. Men the world over fantasized about making love to Germaine; women lived vicariously through her hedonistic escapades.

She was a free spirit, a ravishingly beautiful butterfly born to flit from flower to flower, never lighting anywhere for very long. And that was why her marriage to Philip Wingate, a serious young American architect studying in France under Le Corbusier had proved such a surprise.

After a working summer honeymoon spent at Taliesin, Frank Lloyd Wright's Wisconsin home, the couple had settled down in Philadelphia, where Philip had established a reputation for successfully integrating contemporary buildings into the city's historical landscape. Their marriage of this seemingly incompatible pair had outlasted most of their critics, continuing for thirty-seven years until Philip's death of a heart attack three years before.

After four decades in America Germaine continued to look like a Paris fashion plate and to sound like Jacques Cousteau.

"*Oui*. The big picture," Germaine repeated with an inimitable Gallic self-confidence. "You assist Darius Wilde with his research, allowing him to write his book, and he in turn provides you with an excellent source of publicity. Publicity which certainly can't hurt in your never-ending quest for funding, *n'est-ce pas*?"

"The Peter and Wendy Family Circus and Penguin Extravaganza has all the funding it needs, thank you."

"Rubbish. I happen to have read in this morning's *Wall Street Journal* that Langley Airlines has just gone into receivership; how much did that bankruptcy cost you in lost corporate pledges?"

"A bit," Sara acknowledged reluctantly. "But we've already got it covered," she insisted. All right, so it was a lie; it was only a small white one. "So you see, Germaine, we really don't need whatever minuscule amount of publicity a book with a college press run of five hundred might bring in."

"I could always tell when you were fibbing, *chérie*," the older woman said gently. "And for your information, Darius isn't gearing the book toward a college press; he's writing it for a mass-market audience."

"Writing a book is one thing," Sara pointed out. "Selling it to a reputable publishing house is an entirely different story. How do I know he'll even find anyone interested enough in circuses to publish it?"

"Everyone's interested in circuses, *n'est-ce pas*?" Germaine replied with a graceful shrug. "At least they certainly should be. And on the remote chance the manuscript does happen to land on the desk of some philistine who has never daydreamed about running off to join the circus, Darius's book will certainly change his mind. And while I'm at it, my dear, may I point out that you are behaving terribly out of character by refusing to consider all the ramifications of this project? Since when has Sara McBride developed such a closed mind?"

Sara waited to answer until the waiter had taken away the nearly untouched copper tray and refilled her coffee cup. "Since a woman I've always considered my friend, as well as my godmother, sprang a surprise guest on me," she muttered. "As for ramifications, the only one I see is that I'm going to be stuck all summer with a stuffy old anthropologist who's going to be sticking his long, pointed nose everywhere it doesn't belong."

The older woman appeared unruffled by Sara's mutinous attitude. The only outward sign of her displeasure was the manicured hand that patted her elegantly arranged white hair. The gesture was unnecessary; Germaine, as usual, was impeccably turned out.

"Darius Wilde's nose is neither long nor pointed," she corrected. "I also know of several women who would argue that he's far from stuffy."

"Good. Then let *them* spend the next three and a half months with him."

"He doesn't want them. He wants you."

Sara's frustrated sigh ruffled her coppery bangs. Germaine wasn't a blood relative, although Sara had grown up calling the close family friend Tante Germaine. Over the years, as Sara struggled against the bonds of the conservative Cornell family's expectations, her honorary aunt had frequently served as an intermediary, providing a much-needed bridge between Sara and her often distraught parents.

It had been Germaine who had provided Sara with her long sought-after wish—two weeks at the Ringling Clown College—upon her graduation from Sarah Lawrence. Only Germaine had understood when Sara turned down an excellent offer from a prestigious New York advertising firm in order to organize a group of struggling street performers into a highly touted experimental theater group.

And when Sara's faltering marriage to Jeremy McBride had finally crumbled disastrously around her feet, it had been Germaine who had shown up at the door of Sara's University City apartment with a magnum of Dom Perignon and the suggestion that they "drown the bastard."

Sara loved Germaine Wingate; there wasn't anything she wouldn't do for her. But why, oh, why, she agonized, did it have to be this?

"And what if *I* don't want him?" she challenged softly.

"You haven't even met him," Germaine pointed out. "How can you possibly know how you feel about him?"

Sara dragged her hands through her tumble of red-gold hair. Hands that, Germaine's sharp eyes noted, were trembling visibly.

"After my experience with Jeremy, I developed a built-in radar, like those earthquake predictors they've set up on the San Andreas Fault in California; get me anywhere near anyone even resembling an academician and my needle goes spinning right off the dial."

"Pooh. Darius is hardly your typical academician. He doesn't even smoke a pipe."

"Jeremy didn't smoke a pipe, either."

"That's right, I seem to recall your ex-husband preferring something a bit more exotic, not to mention illegal. Which always made me wonder how on earth he justified his scathing criticisms of your comparatively innocent pursuits."

Good question. And one Sara had asked her husband several times over the course of their distressful three-year marriage. "Jeremy never felt the need to justify his behavior to anyone."

"But he did feel free to criticize yours at the drop of a hat."

"That's about it," Sara agreed glumly.

"Well, you're well rid of him."

"I know."

That they were talking about her former husband, five years after he had walked out on her, only served to underscore Sara's belief that allowing Dr. Darius Wilde, Ph.D., to insinuate his way into her life for three and a half long months would be a mistake of enormous proportions. But how to make Germaine understand was a problem.

She was silent for a moment as she studied her lunch companion. Clad in an ageless gray Chanel suit trimmed with black piping, a single strand of pearls, matching earrings, a simple gold watch and a wide gold wedding band, Germaine Wingate gave the impression that elegance was her natural condition.

Her makeup had been applied with a light, skillful hand and the natural white of her feathered hair softened her features and took years off her age. Not that Germaine Wingate was at all vain about her advancing years; she was currently planning a huge party for her sixty-fifth birthday. Sara had promised to return to Philadelphia in August for the occasion.

Germaine was a great deal more than an attractive, middle-aged woman, Sara decided. She was an elegantly clad bulldozer who could roll over you with such velvet-soft pressure that it didn't seem to hurt at the time, but flattened you nonetheless.

"Why the entire sixteen weeks?" she asked finally.

Germaine's gray eyes brightened to a gleaming silver as she sensed Sara's impending capitulation. "That's how long your tour lasts, *oui*?"

"But can't he get all the facts he needs in a week? Ten days at the most?"

"Dry, boring facts he can get from books," Germaine pointed out, waving her cigarette holder. A thin veil of blue smoke drifted between them before dissipating in the artificially cooled air. "Darius has always preferred to immerse himself fully in his research projects."

Without even knowing the man, Sara felt like immersing Darius Wilde in a vat of boiling oil. He was going to ruin her tour. Sara knew it.

"Tell him to come and see me after Friday's matinee."

"*Et voilà.* Friday it is." Germaine had the good grace not to display her satisfaction. She merely rubbed her hands together as if she had never expected any other outcome.

As they left the restaurant, she kissed Sara on both cheeks. "Believe me, *chérie*, someday you are going to thank me for this."

Sara knew Germaine prided herself on her ability to predict the future. Blessed with what seemed to be second sight, she had certainly proved herself right on more than one occasion where Sara was concerned. Including the time she'd insisted that Sara's impending marriage was doomed to fail, and to bring with it a shattering heartbreak that she would eventually learn to live with, but never quite dispel.

Well, she'd hit that one right on the bull's eye, Sara admitted, even as she felt her heart tighten at the unhappy memories. But this time Germaine was dead wrong. Sara would be just as likely to thank her longtime friend for a plague of locusts.

"SHE WAS absolutely mad about the idea, *chérie*," the woman Darius Wilde had come to think of as his fairy godmother swore over grilled red snapper during a long lunch at La Terrasse the following day.

The restaurant, located near the University of Pennsylvania, was bustling with its usual eclectic clientele: students, business people, academics.

Walking out of his campus office that morning, Darius had felt like an eight-year-old boy on the last day of school. It had been necessary to pull a few strings, but fortunately his sterling reputation in academic circles carried a great deal of weight with the university administration. A teaching assistant had been assigned to take over his classes for the last few weeks of the semester, and a proctor had been appointed to monitor the final exams. If everything went as planned, he was leaving his cramped basement office, rigid schedules and departmental meetings behind him.

September and Labor Day seemed light-years away, summer stretching before him in all its warm golden glory. For the next three and a half months he was going to breathe in the scents of sawdust, greasepaint and caramel corn rather than chalk dust, photocopier fluid and moldy textbooks. Thanks to Germaine Wingate, this latest project was going to be an experience he'd remember for the rest of his life.

"She liked the idea?"

Germaine smiled over the rim of the glass holding her icy vodka gimlet. "Why, I don't have the words to describe her reaction."

Inordinately pleased by her response, he signaled the waitress for another beer as he leaned back in the chair with a deep sigh of relief. When Germaine had first approached him with the idea, he'd been immediately enthusiastic but had confessed doubts that Sara McBride would be willing to have a stranger practically living in her back pocket while the Peter and Wendy Family Circus and Penguin Extravaganza took to the road for its annual tour. Her apparent enthusiasm was bound to make an already stimulating experience even better.

"I don't know how to thank you," he said.

Germaine waved away his appreciation with a delicate flick of her wrist. "Just name the first one after me."

It was noisy enough in the glassed-in terrace that Darius decided he must have misunderstood. "Excuse me?"

Germaine quickly shifted her attention to the nearby ailanthus tree as her mind searched for ways to correct her faux pas. She shouldn't have ordered that second gimlet. But if this wasn't cause for celebration, she didn't know what was.

She had been trying to get these two together for years. The first occasion had been when she'd thrown a gala party for Sara's twenty-first birthday. Unfortunately Darius had chosen that summer to take off to Brazil in order to live among the Kayapo Indians of the Amazon Basin. At that same party Sara had met Jeremy McBride, an unforgivably pompous tutor at Oxford's University College who had been guest lecturing at the University of Pennsylvania.

Once Sara had recovered from her terminated marriage, Germaine's thoughts had again turned to Darius. But the cultural anthropologist was continually away from Philadelphia as he wandered the world— herding cattle with the Masai on the Serengeti Plain of Tanzania, spinning prayer wheels in a monastery with the monks of the Dalai Lama in Tibet, fishing with the Inuit in the icy waters above the Arctic Circle.

At long last Darius appeared to be showing signs of settling down. He'd signed a contract with the University of Pennsylvania that would keep him in Philadelphia for two years—more than enough time to get him and Sara together.

"I merely suggested that you dedicate the book to me," she lied smoothly with a composed expression.

Darius lifted his glass of beer in a silent salute. "I wouldn't think of dedicating it to anyone else."

The older woman's only response was a slight, knowing smile. "Give me your hand," she said unexpectedly.

Darius knew Germaine's proclivity for reading the future, and while the academic side of his mind wanted to reject the idea, his intuitive sense had accepted her unorthodox talent years ago.

"What's the matter, did you leave your crystal ball at home?"

"Don't be sarcastic, *chéri*. It doesn't suit you." She arched a silver brow. "Your hand?"

He extended it across the table, holding back a smile as she traced the lines on his palm with a highly buffed oval fingernail.

"You are an extremely intelligent man, but you have a habit of losing yourself in scholarly pursuits and forgetting about the outside world."

"So try telling me something I don't know."

"You've been searching all these years for something you cannot quite define. Now, perhaps like Dorothy, back from Oz, you are about to discover that the key to happiness has existed all along in your own backyard, *n'est-ce pas*?"

"Germaine, you've been to my loft; the only backyard I have is the alley, and it's currently occupied by a row of battered trash cans and a group of winos who sit around all day drinking Ripple out of brown paper bags."

"I know that you are a scholar, but must you always be so literal?" she chided. "I was, of course, speaking figuratively." Her fingernail skimmed across his palm. "See this? You possess an exceedingly long lifeline, Darius."

"After making it through this last semester with two sections of freshman intro courses on my schedule, I can probably survive anything."

"You're going to have children. Two. *Non*, three."

"You don't happen to see a wife in there anywhere, do you? If I'm going to have three kids, she'd probably come in handy."

"*Oui*, she's there, as well," Germaine confided. "Only one, and you're going to be married for a very long time."

In spite of his lingering skepticism, Darius found the idea oddly appealing. "I'm glad to hear it, especially since divorce is reputed to be rough on the kids."

"Aha, this shows that you have an exciting adventure ahead of you."

"Hey, that's cheating," he complained laughingly. "You already knew about my upcoming adventure because you're the one who set it up."

"You are an extremely intelligent man, Darius. But you must learn to listen to your heart. And not your head."

Her earnest expression was strangely disconcerting. "I'll work on that. How about dessert?" he asked in a not very subtle attempt to change the subject as he retrieved his hand.

Her intense gaze didn't waver from his encouraging one. "Promise me."

Darius reminded himself that everyone was entitled to his or her little idiosyncrasies. After all, he undoubtedly had one or two of his own. "Hey, I promise," he said soothingly.

Germaine banished the unbidden image of Jeremy McBride that had clouded her blissful vision of Darius and Sara, and warmth flooded back into her body as she forced herself to dwell on exactly how perfect these two young people were for one another.

There was, of course, one important thing that Darius would need to know about Sara. But Germaine did not feel it her place to tell him. If things went as she hoped, in time it would be up to Sara to reveal the painful incidents in her past.

"I believe I will have some dessert," she decided. "Although I'll have to run an extra mile this evening to work off the calories."

His judicious gaze swept over the still-beautiful woman and Darius found himself wishing that he were thirty years older. Or that she were thirty years younger. Germaine Wingate was an attractive, compelling woman, even at sixty-four, and if he ever met anyone who intrigued him half as much as she did, he'd marry her on the spot.

"You're perfect, just the way you are."

"Why, *merci*, Darius. And although I am flattered by your desire to dispense with the difference in years, your time would be much better spent seeking someone closer to your own age."

Darius had seen Germaine's psychic powers in action too many times over the years to discount their validity. Still, he was admittedly shaken by her apparent ability to read his mind. A small frisson of something he couldn't quite define skimmed up his spine as she turned away to signal their waitress.

APPEARANCES, Sara McBride reminded herself two days after her lunch with Germaine, could be deceiving.

Take this afternoon, for example: the spring day was alive with golden sunshine, sawdust, fresh popped corn and magic. The wonderful cacophony of a calliope hidden behind the blue-and-white canvas drifted on the breeze, adding to the building sense of anticipation among the crowd and performers alike.

Tow-haired children wiggled atop tall stools, giggling as white-faced clowns emblazoned their foreheads with silver stars and painted jagged lightning bolts across their freckled cheeks. Adolescent boys wearing T-shirts bearing the names of their favorite rock groups—U-2, Bon Jovi, Psychedelic Furs—threw baseball after baseball at maddeningly stubborn bowling pins while nearby, a twelve-year-old girl had better luck pitching dimes into goldfish bowls.

Teenagers strolled down the midway in search of other teenagers, their poses studiously nonchalant, as if to demonstrate that they were too sophisticated to actually enjoy such infantile forms of entertainment. A pair of senior citizens sat holding hands on a painted wooden bench, smiling, remembering.

No one observing the carefree, idyllic scene would have any reason to suspect it was the site of impending conflict. Indeed, it was a tribute to Sara's acting ability that not one of the individuals she stopped to chat with realized how upset she was. She had no way of knowing that the object of all her angst was only a few feet away, making copious notes in a small black note-book.

An hour later there was a flare of trumpets. And then it began.

The *grand charivari*: there were fanfares as people dressed in gaily colored tights and bright spangles ran around the ring waving flags. Jugglers juggled, tumblers tumbled, clowns clowned. It was chaos. Confusion. Insanity. It was blinding flash and dazzling beauty. Watching from a seat at the top of the bright blue bleachers, Darius decided that the show fell somewhere between recess at a school for the terminally hyperactive and a fire drill.

For the next two hours, he watched as the performers—ordinary people who had been magically transformed into something extraordinary—tossed an amazing number of balls, clubs and rings at one another. Clowns tripped on slick yellow banana peels and fell, as they'd been doing for centuries, and when the audience roared its approval, they struggled gamely to their feet only to fall again. A woman clad in red spangles jumped so high on a trampoline that it seemed she would disappear into the puffy white clouds; a man dressed in a gorilla suit and top hat walked on his hands across a taut wire.

The oohs and aahs of the crowd competed with the upbeat and celebratory sound of the orchestra, and when it was over, the people reluctantly drifted away, talking excitedly to one another about the magic they'd witnessed. But as they left, they took some of the magic with them; a small part of the circus would stay forever in their minds and hearts.

It was the reaction of the audience, as much as the obvious camaraderie of the performers, that assured Darius he'd made the right decision. The Peter and Wendy Family Circus and Penguin Extravaganza was the most inventive show of its kind, a rare theatrical treat.

The book he had in mind was not only going to be a pleasure to write, but also, as long as he succeeded in capturing the magic and diversity of the troupe of traveling players, it should prove a delight to read.

As he walked toward the large tent at the edge of the midway, Darius was smiling to himself in anticipation of the weeks to come.

2

IT HAD GONE WELL. Better than well, Sara decided. The audience had loved them. If the rest of the performances were even a tenth as successful, she would consider the tour a smashing success.

Basking in a warm feeling of satisfaction, she had almost forgotten about Darius Wilde. Then she made the mistake of glancing up into the large makeup mirror in the main tent and saw the tall, dark-haired man standing in the opening where the tent flap had been turned back.

He stood very straight; his unbending bearing appeared to be his natural manner rather than the result of any conscious desire to intimidate. His face was dark and lean, with angular planes and shadows, and his eyes, as he looked searchingly around the interior of the tent, were nearly as dark as the straight black hair that flowed to the top of his shirt collar. He was the most intriguing, yet unsettling, man Sara had ever seen.

When those dark eyes sought her out, seeming to hold her curious gaze in the mirror by sheer strength of will, she felt a sudden tightening in her stomach.

Don't be ridiculous, she told herself as she forced herself to rise slowly, deliberately, from the folding chair. *He's probably from the city, here to check our permit; just one more bureaucrat who earns a living creating the unending tangle of red tape the rest of us have to fight our way through every day.*

Granted, he didn't look like a bureaucrat. But, Sara reminded herself for the second time this afternoon, appearances were often deceiving.

"May I help you?"

"I'm looking for Sara McBride." His lips were finely chiseled and severe. Sara found herself wondering if they would soften when he smiled.

She wiped her hand on her skirt before extending it with a cautious smile of her own. "Congratulations. You've just found her."

Darius stared down at the woman whose hand had just disappeared into his much larger one. Sara McBride's narrow face was surrounded by an enormous Afro wig dyed myriad Day-Glo colors. Round circles the color and size of Red Delicious apples had been painted on her cheeks, and her curly black eyelashes were at least six inches long.

Her hands and face hinted that she'd be slim under her costume, but it was impossible to tell for sure. There was enough material in the orange-and-purple paisley dress to make the world's most gaudy parachute, and her high-topped, black-and-orange basketball sneakers were at least a size eighteen. As he continued to scrutinize her outlandish appearance, Darius was aware on some distant plane of being rude, but he couldn't help himself.

"Darius Wilde," he said distractedly as he attempted to locate the woman behind the garishly clad clown. "I believe we had an appointment."

Her attitude abruptly turned icy. "So you came after all. I wasn't certain you would."

The chill in her tone contrasted sharply with her appearance—a disconcerting combination of Mae West, Miss Piggy and a bowery bag lady. Darius wondered why Germaine had not warned him ahead of time that Sara McBride was not an average, run-of-the-mill circus manager, then decided that she'd probably thought it would be fun to shake him out of his musty academic abstraction. There were times, he thought, that Germaine's sense of humor left a great deal to be desired.

"I wouldn't miss it for the world," he said truthfully.

Damn. His voice was every bit as smooth and dark as his eyes. Sara didn't know who she was more furious with—Germaine for coming up with this ridiculous idea or herself for agreeing to it.

"You're not at all what I expected," he offered as an uncomfortable silence settled around them.

Her eyes, framed by those absurd lashes, narrowed as Sara looked him up and down slowly and deliberately. He was casually dressed in a blue chambray shirt, the sleeves of which he'd rolled to the elbow, and a pair of well-worn jeans that were faded at the seams. On his feet were a pair of scuffed, utilitarian cowboy boots. He was very different from most of the academics she'd met. And worlds away from Jeremy. That Darius Wilde's appearance inspired unwelcome memories of her former husband made Sara all the more determined to dislike him.

"Then we're even. Because you're not at all what I expected, either." She chewed thoughtfully on a short thumbnail. "Did you leave the rumpled chinos and clip-on bow tie at home, professor?"

He wondered what it was about Sara McBride that had him admiring her when he should have been offended. Perhaps it was the way she managed to appear dignified while clad in a dress bulky enough to conceal the Liberty Bell. Or perhaps it was the unspoken challenge hovering in those unbelievably blue eyes.

Or perhaps it was something else entirely. Something he couldn't quite put his finger on. Yet.

"That bad, huh?"

She shrugged. "I'd be less than honest if I told you that I'm delighted with Tante Germaine's latest brainstorm."

Once again Darius was forced to wonder exactly what Germaine had gotten him into. "Tante Germaine? She's your aunt?"

"Not exactly. She's been a close friend of the family since before I was born. She's also my godmother. In many ways I've felt closer to her than my own parents."

"How old are you?" he surprised them both by asking.

"Twenty-nine. Why?"

"Just a thought I had." There were four years between Sara McBride and himself. Recalling Germaine's advice about finding a woman nearer his own age, he recognized what appeared to be a complex matchmaking scheme. Darius decided, in an attempt to postpone the start of World War III, not to let Sara in on their mutual friend's treachery until he had smoothed the waters a bit.

But that didn't stop his mind from working overtime as he attempted to get a mental image of what Sara would look like without that outlandish costume. Her eyes—the color of a sun-brightened alpine lake—suggested that her hair, under that fluorescent wig, would be light. Either blond or red, he decided. Her fair complexion along with the sprinkling of freckles across the bridge of her nose made him suspect it would have more of a tawny hue.

"So when did you want to get started?" she asked with a decided lack of enthusiasm. "I suppose you have some questions concerning the logistics of the tour."

Darius supposed it was an encouraging sign that she hadn't yet tried to throw him out of the park. "How about right now?" he suggested with a hint of a smile that perversely made Sara want to see more. "I'd like to get some background on the Peter and Wendy Family Circus and Penguin Extravaganza."

She needed time. Time to absorb the fact that in those first few seconds Darius Wilde had stirred something in her. An awareness that she hadn't felt for a long, long time.

Sara was an individual who ran on emotions. There had been a time, not so many years ago, when she'd waged daily battles against the often tumultuous feelings that had been the bane of her family's existence.

Those same emotions had contributed, albeit indirectly, to the downfall of her marriage. But Sara had since come to terms with her demonstrative nature, utilizing her wide range of feelings in her work.

Although she knew that most people thought of a clown as nothing more than a clumsy fool in whiteface and big shoes, Sara believed in presenting feelings deep inside herself that needed purging. When she offered those feelings to her audience, they experienced them, as well, and through an often mystifying transference, managed to purge their own doubts and fears, turning them into something less frightening, less threatening.

Believing this, Sara accepted that the more open and childlike she remained, the more effective she could be in her work. The problem with such a philosophy was that sometimes a person found herself face-to-face with emotions that were decidedly unsettling. And potentially dangerous. Like now. The feelings that Darius Wilde had stirred were precisely those from which a wary woman would retreat.

"Sorry," she said after a pause, "but I've just enough time before the evening performance to catch a quick bite and blow up some new balloons for the opening number."

"How about after that? We can discuss it over a late supper."

Sara shook her Day-Glo head. "I'm really sorry, but I can't. It's my parents' thirty-fifth wedding anniversary, and I promised my father that I wouldn't be too late." The memory of Richard Cornell's stern lecture concerning time and familial responsibilities intruded on an already uncomfortable moment. "It's sort of a command performance."

"Thirty-five years is a long time."

"Isn't it?" She pulled the wig off, releasing a tumbled cloud of red-gold hair. Darius experienced an instant tightening in his body that he recognized as desire, then carefully restrained it.

Sara was suddenly looking at him with renewed interest. "You wouldn't happen to be an art expert, would you?"

"Sorry."

"Don't be. You're just the person I've been looking for. Everyone around here seems to think they're a critic for the *New York Times*, or something equally stuffy. I'll be back in a jiff. Don't go away."

"I wouldn't think of it."

As he waited for her return, Darius wondered what Germaine had been thinking of, pairing him with Sara McBride. The women who succeeded in luring him away from his work from time to time were sleek, intelligent and coolly sophisticated. Women at home in drawing rooms smelling of hothouse flowers, furniture oil and expensive perfumes. This wide-eyed waif with the tousled clouds of coppery hair was a clown. Her milieu was sawdust and greasepaint. If she was still trying to marry him off, Germaine could not have found a more unlikely candidate if she tried.

Entranced in spite of himself, Darius remained where he was, watching as two clowns dressed in top hats and tails practiced walking up a collapsing staircase. In the corner of the tent a lithe young woman was standing on her head, twirling a barbell with her feet. Another young woman walked by on stilts, carrying a baby in a canvas pouch, while a man wearing the tail end of a donkey suit played Go Fish with a dark-haired child Darius took to be his son.

The amazing thing about it was that no one seemed to think their actions at all out of the ordinary. Darius was beginning to feel as if he'd just fallen down the rabbit hole.

"Here it is," Sara announced, returning to the tent with a bulky package.

"Interesting gift wrap, for a wedding anniversary."

"Isn't it?" she agreed cheerfully, putting aside her earlier irritation as she studied the bright paper. "I've always adored Garfield. It's too bad we'll have to tear it, but if we don't, you won't be able to see what's inside, will you?"

Darius pulled a Swiss Army knife out of the front pocket of his jeans. "Let me," he suggested, just as she appeared ready to wreak havoc with the cartoon cat-covered paper.

"I should have known." Sara sighed as she handed him the package and stepped back.

Darius methodically slit the tape. "Known what?"

"I came to the conclusion a very long time ago that there are two kinds of people in the world. Neat ones and not-so-neat ones. And unwrapping presents is probably one of the best ways to sort them out." She watched as he folded back the gift wrap. "I should have known you'd be one of the neat ones."

He glanced up at her. "Why do I get the impression I've just been insulted?"

"You're perceptive, too," she murmured. "But then, I suppose I should have suspected that. From a scholar."

Darius was on the verge of complaining about her seeming penchant for stereotypes when he made the mistake of looking down at Sara's anniversary gift. It was a large oil painting, simply framed in a museum-quality aluminum frame. But it was the startling subject matter that captured his attention. Bold flashes of cobalt blue streaked across the snow-white canvas like jagged lightning bolts hurled from the hand of Thor. Although he was admittedly no expert on art, Darius suspected that the effort was amateurish, at best. But there was no denying that there was an incredible amount of energy in the painting.

"You painted this, didn't you?" he asked, already knowing the answer.

"Guilty," Sara agreed with a quick, strangely self-conscious grin. "It's an abstract seascape; I wanted to do a sunrise—my mother adores getting up early to watch the sun rise, something I've never been able to understand, even though I'm usually up before the birds myself, but of course that's only due to necessity—but anyway, unfortunately I waited until the very last minute, and then, although I searched everywhere, all I could find around the house was that bright blue paint. I suppose it all turned out for the best. My parents' bedroom is decorated in blues and Mr. Olson at the frame shop told me that the thirty-fifth anniversary is coral, and since coral comes from the sea, this painting is absolutely perfect."

When she smiled—really smiled—Darius had the feeling that Mr. Olson, whoever he was, would consider anything this woman did to be absolutely perfect.

"So," Sara asked, finally stopping long enough to take a much-needed breath, "what do you think?"

It was a test and they both knew it. Darius returned his attention to the vivid canvas, receiving what felt like an electrical jolt as its intense, unrestrained passion hit him directly in the midsection.

"I think," he said slowly, carefully, "that it would be impossible for anyone to fall asleep with this hanging on their bedroom wall."

Sara had her choice. She could take his words as either a compliment or an insult. She opted for the former. "What a nice thing to say. And just when I was trying so hard not to like you, too."

"Does this mean you've changed your mind about not wanting my company?"

She was silent for a moment as she gave him a long, appraising look. Despite his outwardly amiable demeanor, she suspected that this was a man who knew precisely what he wanted out of life and was accustomed to achieving it. There was something in those cool, dark eyes—something she still hadn't quite put a finger on—that led her to suspect that Darius Wilde would not be an easy person to handle. But it was that same underlying sense of tightly restrained power that made him so undeniably intriguing.

Oh, Germaine, Sara thought. *You've always known that I could never resist a puzzle.*

"No. It means that if my parents are horrified by their present this evening, I'm giving it to you." Abandoning her dislike of him for the moment, Sara permitted her amusement to show in her eyes.

"You've got yourself a deal," he agreed, accepting her challenge. "And in the event your parents decide to keep your masterpiece, you can simply paint another one. To hang on my bedroom wall."

"You wouldn't get much sleep," she warned.

He shrugged. "You could keep me company on those long, sleepless nights."

For all of her twenty-nine years, Sara had followed her instincts with mixed results. Changing her major from business to theater during her junior year in college had turned out well; Jeremy, of course, had been an unmitigated disaster. Establishing the NewMarket Players had been described by local critics as both daring and brilliant, and when she'd borrowed the much-needed capital to take those same multitalented performers and their imaginative show on the road, the traveling circus had proven immensely popular.

The same inner voice that had counseled her to transform a small group of independent street performers into a critically acclaimed touring company was now telling her that once she allowed Darius Wilde into her life, that life would be inexorably altered.

For better or for worse, she couldn't yet guess. Sara knew that a sensible woman would turn away from temptation now, before things got out of hand. A pru-

dent woman would suggest that he find himself some
other project. But no one had ever described Sara as
being either a sensible or prudent woman.

She made her mind up quickly because that was her
nature. "Since I'm not into performing art, you'll have
to find someone else to keep you company in bed, Dr.
Wilde. However, if you're still interested in traveling
with us, meet me at General Hospital tomorrow evening around six and we'll talk about logistics."

"General Hospital?"

"Tomorrow's Saturday," she said, as if that explained everything.

"I see," he murmured, not seeing anything at all.

"I always perform at the hospital on Saturdays."

"I'll be there. Where shall I meet you?"

Sara glanced around distractedly as a deep, masculine voice called her name. Darius's gaze followed hers
across the tent to a muscular blond man who had held
the audience spellbound with his skill on the high wire.
When Sara beamed in response and waved, something
moved deep inside him. Something dark and unfamil-
iar.

"I'm sorry to cut this getting-to-know-you chat short,
but I really do have to run," she said, not looking the
slightest bit regretful. "I promised Kevin I'd work on a
new act with him."

When the man called her again, Darius managed,
with effort, to squelch his irritation. "Where?" he repeated.

"We're going to rehearse right outside. Why?"

"Where should I meet you at the hospital?" he clarified with uncommon patience. "What floor?"

"Oh. Just ask anyone," she suggested airily, retrieving the painting from him. "I'm always easy to track down. Oh, and Darius?"

"Yes?"

"Thank you for lying about the painting. It was a very nice thing to do." With that she was gone, moving with a lithe, careless grace that made him wish he could strip off that oversize, padded dress and view the real Sara McBride.

As Darius watched Sara link arms with the tightrope walker and leave the tent, laughing merrily at something the man had said, he reluctantly recognized that previously undefined emotion as jealousy.

He stood in the open flap of the red-and-white canvas tent for a long, silent time, breathing in the scents of greasepaint and sawdust and popcorn as he stared after her.

ANGIE ANGOTTI HAD long, silky black hair and big brown eyes the color of Swiss chocolate. That she was also encased in thick white plaster from her shoulders to her toes was something that the seven-year-old girl was taking with a great deal more equanimity than her harried mother. Mrs. Angotti was hovering nervously nearby, looking for all the world like a fretful, plump hummingbird.

"I knew it was a mistake to take this one to see *Peter Pan*," the woman muttered in accented English. She wrung her hands, as if she expected her daughter to leap up from the narrow bed, race over to the third-story window and make yet another unsuccessful attempt to fly.

But she need not have worried. It was doubtful Angie would manage to escape all the pulleys and weights that were keeping her broken young body in traction, especially when her attention was presently riveted on Sara McBride. As was Darius Wilde's.

The young patients in Philadelphia General Hospital thought Sara was the funniest woman they'd ever met. Having spent the past two hours watching Sara clown her way through the wards, Darius had the impression the parents of the children she entertained every Saturday considered her the most beautiful. That she loved her work was obvious. That she loved these children was even more so.

"All right," Sara challenged them, as her slender hands manipulated a sky-blue balloon into an intricate shape, "who does this remind you of?"

Angie's dark eyes danced with glee as she recognized the balloon figure immediately. "It's Dr. Friedman!"

Sara looked with feigned surprise at the balloon in her hands and then at the short, rotund resident standing beside Darius in the open doorway. "Why, good gracious, so it is." Her enormous scarlet mouth stretched even further as she handed the caricature to the perpetually cheerful young doctor.

"I'll treasure this always," he promised gravely.

Sara fluttered her outrageously long lashes and gave him a syrupy look that Scarlet O'Hara would have envied. "Why, Dr. Friedman, aren't you just the sweetest little ol' thing?" she drawled.

"Oh-oh," Angie cried out, "better watch out, Dr. Friedman; Sassy Sally's making cow eyes again."

Sara pressed her hand against her chest. *"Moi?"* she asked innocently. All the children knew that Sassy Sally—Sara's Saturday-afternoon alter ego—was a scandalous flirt.

The electronic pager hooked to the resident's belt suddenly buzzed. "Saved by the bell." He wiped his brow with exaggerated relief. "Do me a favor and keep this for me, will you?" he asked Angie as he placed the ballroom figure on the table beside her bed.

"Sure. And you can visit it anytime you want."

He winked a twinkling dark eye. "You've got yourself a deal, kiddo." The pager buzzed again. Tossing the little girl a kiss, Dr. Friedman hurried out of the room.

As she watched the resident leave, Sara found herself momentarily trapped by Darius's brooding, speculative gaze. She was determined not to make it easy on him, and some perverse emotion made her stick out her tongue. Instead of falling mortally wounded to the floor, or appearing properly shocked, as she'd hoped he might, Darius merely raised a dark brow and continued staring at her.

As she looked back into his eyes, Sara envied his ability to hide his thoughts so well. Her own face had always mirrored her every emotion.

Stifling a small sigh, Sara returned her attention to the little girl. "Try to guess this one," she challenged as she blew up two more balloons—one yellow, one pink—and twisted them together.

Faint lines furrowed Angie's smooth olive brow as she studied the new figure. Her eyes were as gravely serious as if she were attempting to unravel the secrets of relativity single-handedly.

"It's a rabbit," she said finally. "No, not a rabbit. An airplane." She frowned. "No, a rabbit."

"Both are half right," Sara announced. "This is a very special animal found only in the most remote regions of the world. Like New Zealand. Or Timbuktu. Or Philadelphia."

"What is it?" Angie shouted. If she'd been able to move her arms, she would have clapped her hands.

Sara grinned. "Can't you tell? It's a hare-plane, silly!"

Angie dissolved into silvery giggles. Even Mrs. Angotti managed a smile, the first Sara had seen on her face in the four weeks she'd been visiting the little girl.

Sara placed the balloon hare-plane beside the blue resident on the table. Then she bent and brushed her lips lightly against the child's smooth cheek. "Gotta go, sweetie."

"Do you have to?"

"I really do." Sara looked down into Angie's limpid dark eyes and decided that if she skipped dinner and fudged the speed limit on the Ben Franklin Parkway by five or ten miles per hour, she could stay an additional five minutes and still make it back to Fairmont Park in time to help the crew strike the show.

"Just one more trick," she said.

"One more." Angie's knowing grin revealed she'd known all along that Sara would give in. As she always did.

Sara ruffled the little girl's dark hair affectionately. "My goodness, what do we have here?" When she pulled an enormous bouquet of paper flowers from behind Angie's ear, the child's eyes lit up as if she'd just been given a deed to her very own diamond mine. "Flowers for the prettiest girl on the floor," Sara declared, tucking them under a blue sheet emblazoned with vintage airplanes.

Usually such sheets were assigned to male patients, with little girls preferring Strawberry Shortcake or Rainbow Brite. But when Sara discovered Angie's penchant for flying, she had promptly raided the linen closet on the second floor. Instead of being annoyed with Sara's meddling in hospital procedures, the head nurse for the ward had left instructions that Angie would continue to receive the airplane sheets for as long as she was in the hospital.

Sara and Darius had just reached the elevator when Mrs. Angotti caught up with them. "I want to thank you for being so nice to my Angie."

"Angie's easy to be nice to."

"She's a terror."

Sara recalled her own childhood, knowing she'd been the bane of her parents' staid, proper existence. "Probably. But she's one of the nicest terrors I've ever met."

"God was playing a practical joke on me when he made Angie; that girl gives me gray hairs."

"She also gives you love."

The woman's well-padded shoulders lifted in an expressive shrug that began at the waist. "That, too." Her eyes narrowed as she studied the tall, dark-haired man standing beside Sara with undisguised interest. Her gaze went back and forth between them before returning to Sara. "Do you have any babies?"

Sara struggled against the smothering grief that rose from somewhere deep inside her at the innocent question. "No." Sara pushed the down button for the elevator, eager to escape what she knew was about to become a too personal conversation.

"But you'd like to," Mrs. Angotti persisted.

Although she refused to look at him, she could feel Darius's interested gaze on her face. "Well, yes. I suppose. Someday," she murmured, schooling her voice to a nonchalance she was a very long way from feeling.

"So is this your husband?"

"I'm not married." Sara pushed the button again, in the unlikely event it would cause the car to arrive sooner.

"Then he's a friend?" Mrs. Angotti asked as her expressive dark eyes looked approvingly at Darius. It was obvious that the woman was consumed with curiosity; she'd been casting surreptitious glances toward the silently observant man the entire time Sara had been entertaining her daughter.

"Mrs. Angotti, Darius Wilde." What on earth was keeping the damn elevator?

"I'm so very happy to meet a friend of Sara's," the woman said enthusiastically.

"He's merely an acquaintance. Not a friend," Sara insisted before Darius could respond.

"Not yet perhaps," Darius agreed. "But I'm working on it." His calm, self-assured tone suggested that he hadn't a single doubt about his eventual success.

"Sara is a wonderful girl," Mrs. Angotti continued, unabashed by Sara's antipathy. "And so good with children."

Sara had seen that look before. It was the look that Napoleon, Germaine's bull terrier, got on its pug face just before it grabbed the mailman's pant leg and refused to let go. And it was the same look her mother got every time she invited Sara to dinner to meet one of her friends' lawyer/doctor/stockbroker sons.

"Where is that elevator?" she complained, casting a quick, desperate look down at her wide-banded Mickey Mouse watch. She wanted, more than anything to escape before Mrs. Angotti shifted into overdrive. She punched the elevator button yet again, but it was too late.

"Sara would make a wonderful wife for some lucky man," Angie's mother suggested with a wide, guileless smile.

It was Napoleon all over again. "Really, Mrs. Angotti," Sara murmured.

The woman patted Sara's hand. "You are a nice girl, Sara, but you work too hard." The woman's sly, silky voice was a dead ringer for that of Sara's mother when she got onto this particular topic. Or Germaine's, for that matter. "You should be married, and having babies with your husband. Before you get too old."

Sara felt as if she'd just aged twenty years in two minutes. "I'll keep that in mind." She breathed a sigh of relief as the elevator door finally opened, allowing her to make her escape from Angie's well-intentioned mother.

3

"NOT ONE WORD," Sara warned as she jabbed the button for the ground floor.

Darius crossed his arms over his chest and leaned against the wall next to her. "I wouldn't think of it."

"She's Italian. They're known for their romanticism."

He nodded. "So I hear."

Although his expression remained bland, Sara thought she detected a hint of laughter in his tone. She directed her gaze toward the numbers flashing above the door. "It's just that she's never seen me with a man before, so when you showed up, her imagination ran away with her."

"Makes sense to me," he said. "But if you want to know the truth, I think I like the idea of being the first man you've brought here."

His smile was wry, and far too appealing. She'd thought his lips might soften somewhat when he smiled. But she'd never suspected that they could make her wonder what they'd feel like skimming over her skin. Sara shook off the unwelcome fantasy, reminding herself that she was an intelligent, competent woman, able to handle any situation that came along.

Almost any, she corrected, as painful memories suddenly flooded into her mind. Unbidden visions of her former husband flashed jerkily, like scenes from a silent movie. Jeremy dressed in a gray cutaway on the day of their wedding, Jeremy ensconced in the stacks of the university library, Jeremy awkwardly holding Amy...

Amy. For a horrible, frozen moment the memory of her daughter made Sara feel as if she were drowning. She heard someone calling her name and struggled to concentrate, but the deep, vaguely familiar voice sounded as if it were coming from the bottom of the sea.

"Sara... are you all right?"

His hands were cupping her shoulders, and those dark eyes were staring down into hers. She blinked. Once. Twice. Then once again.

"Excuse me?" she murmured through lips that felt like stone.

"I asked if you were all right."

"Oh. Yes. I'm fine."

His thumbs brushed along her collarbone. Underneath the vivid material her skin burned. "You were trembling."

Deciding that discretion was definitely the better part of valor, Sara forced a bland tone. "Low blood sugar," she assured him shakily as the elevator reached the ground floor and the steel doors opened. "All I need is a candy bar and I'll be fine."

Darius didn't answer immediately. Instead, he continued to study her thoughtfully. Her complexion had gone from attractively pale to ashen, and her blue eyes, which now were gradually clearing, had clouded with a pain so intense it was a wonder that she hadn't cried out.

"What you need is dinner," he said, deciding that this was no time to push.

"Is that an invitation?"

"We haven't discussed the tour," he reminded her as they walked out of the hospital. "It only makes sense to discuss the ground rules over dinner."

"Ground rules?" Sara had never been particularly fond of rules.

"So we can make it through the next sixteen weeks with a minimum of friction."

"Why don't you stay in Philadelphia?" she countered. "That way we can make it through the summer without any friction at all. As for dinner, I'm not hungry."

"You've got a long tour ahead of you; you should eat something to keep up your strength."

His calm, authoritative tone was her undoing, releasing a flood of ancient memories, none of them pleasant. She whirled on him. "What I eat, or not eat, is absolutely none of your business, Dr. Wilde. So why don't you go dig up some bones or something?"

He'd definitely hit a nerve. Curious as to what he could have said to cause that renewed flash of pain in her clear blue eyes Darius reluctantly decided that this was neither the time nor the place to probe.

"I believe you have me confused with an archaeologist," he replied mildly, as if her heated outburst had never occurred. "They dig up the bones. I'm a cultural anthropologist. I specialize in acculturation. The ability of a group of people to assimilate into a larger, more advanced culture," he elaborated at her blank look.

"Oh?" she asked uninterestedly. "And what, exactly, does a cultural anthropologist dig up?"

"If I'm lucky, and I usually am, a better understanding of where we've been. And where we're going."

She frowned at his easy, self-confident tone. "I can already tell you where we're going," she snapped. "We're beginning first thing tomorrow right here in Philadelphia; three and a half months from now we'll end up in Venice, California. If you need any more details, I'd be happy to give you a road map. If you're searching for juicy material for your book, professor, you are definitely digging in the wrong place."

Darius watched the color rise in her fair complexion, rivaling the painted circles on her cheeks in hue and intensity, and was fascinated.

"Thanks for the warning." His gaze remained steady on hers. "I'll keep it in mind."

"You do that."

He inclined his dark head in a brief, accepting nod. "I will. Now that we've got that out of the way, how about dinner?"

It was only dinner. And she was starving. "All right. But I want to change my clothes before we eat. When I go out in this outfit, everyone seems to expect me to remain in character."

"That must get tiring."

"Exhausting," she agreed, halting in front of a fire-engine-red hatchback.

"So we'll stop by your house on the way to the restaurant."

"I'd rather just meet you there."

"Why don't I just come with you?" he suggested.

Sara glanced around the parking lot. "And leave your car in the parking lot?"

"That's not a problem; I gave it away for the summer."

"You did what?"

"Gave my car away."

"Why?"

He shrugged. "A friend of mine recently returned home from living for six months on one of the more remote islands of the Philippines, documenting the gathering techniques of a group of near-Stone Age natives, only to discover that her husband had moved out of their apartment."

"There's a lot of that going around," Sara agreed dryly. "But what does that have to do with your giving away your car?"

"Peter's moving out was the good news; the guy was definitely a jerk. We all wondered why Laura put up with him as long as she did. The bad news was that the jerk also absconded with the stereo, the microwave, every one of her Buddy Holly albums and the Volvo."

"So you gave her your car."

"Only for the summer. She needed transportation; my car needed to be driven to keep it in running order. And since I'm not going to be in Philadelphia this summer—"

There was one thing this man had in common with Jeremy after all, Sara decided grimly. They were both self-confident to the point of arrogance. "Pretty sure of yourself, aren't you, Dr. Wilde?" she interrupted with a dark frown.

Undercurrents. They were all around them, dark and dangerous, making what should have been a casual conversation extraordinarily difficult. Darius deftly avoided them.

"So I've been told," he answered simply, his studiously bland expression revealing none of his escalating frustration. "Does that bother you?"

Sara gave him a long look, reminding herself of all the things in his favor. Germaine adored him—that much had been obvious. And Germaine, second sight or not, had always been an excellent judge of character. Besides, how many men did she know who'd give away their cars? Even for the summer.

"What kind of car is it?" she challenged.

"A Porsche. Why?"

"Damn. I was hoping it was a junker."

"Why?"

"Because that way your gesture wouldn't seem so altruistic. I don't know many men who would hand over the keys to their Porsche."

"It's six years old," he offered. "Does that help you dislike me?"

She laughed then, the silvery sound reminding Darius of a soft breeze riffling through crystal wind chimes. "Dammit, Darius," she protested, "I really don't want to like you."

"Because you feel Germaine forced me on you?"

"That's one of the reasons," she agreed.

"What's the other?"

She eyed him steadily over the top of the car. "None of your business."

"Even if it concerns me?"

The annoyance in his voice registered with her, but Sara refused to be intimidated. "Especially if it concerns you." She opened the car door and climbed in, gesturing to Darius to do the same.

As she pulled the car out of the hospital parking lot, Darius decided that this was as good a time as any to clear the air. They were scheduled to leave tomorrow morning. He had a lot of work ahead of him and not much time to accomplish it; one thing he didn't intend to do was waste precious time arguing with the lovely but decidedly prickly Sara McBride.

"You really don't want me riding along on this year's tour, do you?"

"I believe that we've already determined that you're perceptive." She cast a quick glance in the rearview mirror before zooming past a delivery truck that was moving more slowly.

"Is it because you resent Germaine's less-than-subtle matchmaking?"

"So you admit to knowing what she's up to?" she asked, downshifting as she approached an intersection.

"Not in the beginning. It only sank in when you told me how old you were."

She shot him a quick look. "What does my age have to do with anything?"

"She's been after me to get married for years," he explained pleasantly. "Then, right after assuring me that you're wild about the idea of my writing a book about your circus, she happened to mention that I should find a woman my own age."

"She told you that I was wild about the idea?" Sara asked incredulously.

"I believe the exact expression she used was 'absolutely mad' about the idea."

"The words fit, but the meaning was definitely twisted to suit her own nefarious purposes," Sara grumbled.

"So I discovered when you greeted me as if I were Jack the Ripper," Darius agreed. "Still, you can't deny that Germaine's done us both a favor."

"I'm not in the market for a husband."

"Nor I a wife. But I know how dependent the Peter and Wendy Family Circus and Penguin Extravaganza is on grants and donations. A book proclaiming your many virtues couldn't hurt."

"That's what Germaine said."

"And as angry as you may be about her meddling in our personal lives, she was right about that. Besides, I've already spent the publisher's advance on some much-needed repairs to my loft. So it looks as if you're stuck with me."

Sara shot him a quick, speculative glance as the car idled at a red light. "How can you sell a book you haven't written?"

"I sold it on the basis of an opening chapter and a synopsis."

"To whom?"

When he named a mass-market hardback publisher, Sara didn't bother to conceal her disbelief. "I find it difficult to believe that they'd actually go to contract on a single chapter."

"And a synopsis," he reminded her.

"Even so . . ."

She certainly wasn't going to be that easy to impress, Darius decided, hearing the skepticism in her voice. Although he might not be in the same class as Stephen King or Robert Ludlum, his book on Laplanders' hunting techniques had received critical acclaim.

And his most recent effort—an in-depth study of the oral tradition of storytelling in black South Africa, which included several never-before-documented folktales—had gone into a sixth printing. It had also garnered him appearances on *The Today Show* and *Nightline*.

"Let's just say that the editor has heard of my work," he said simply.

The light turned green. Sara ignored it, concentrating instead on Darius's confident gaze. One of these days, after she cooled down, she was going to let Germaine know exactly what she thought of this latest scheme of hers.

"All right, but since you're the one with the advance, it's only fair that you buy dinner." An irritated driver in a Mercedes behind them sounded his horn.

Sara glanced into the rearview mirror but didn't move the car.

"I can't think of anything I'd enjoy more than buying you dinner," he agreed easily.

"All right." She shifted into first gear and the car shot across the intersection like a speeding bullet, leaving the Mercedes half a block behind. "Prepare to break the limit on your American Express card, professor."

"My American Express card doesn't have a limit."

She shot him a grin so quick that Darius almost believed he had imagined it. "After tonight they might just decide to give you one," she warned.

He smiled, but intent on weaving through the downtown traffic, Sara missed it.

"IT'LL ONLY TAKE ME twenty minutes to change and get out of this makeup," she promised as she pulled up to the curb in front of her Society Hill home.

Society Hill had been named for the Free Society of Traders, a group of businessmen and investors persuaded by William Penn to settle there with their families in 1683. Although the society didn't survive, the neighborhood did, and during Colonial times it became home to Philadelphia's upper crust. In later years the area, like many urban neighborhoods, fell upon hard times. Fortunately a massive urban renewal project had succeeded in reversing Society Hill's fortunes.

Sara's house had been painstakingly restored to its Colonial charm: its red brick walls were covered with lush green ivy, white shutters bracketed the windows and red and pink geraniums bloomed in window boxes.

Darius decided that the cheery exterior suited her perfectly.

"Fine. That'll give me time to make reservations."

"Oh, we won't need reservations," she said blithely as she rummaged through the enormous gold shoulder bag that was part of Sassy Sally's garish ensemble. "One of these days I'm going to get around to putting my house key and my car key on the same ring," she promised herself.

"That's a good idea," he agreed as he eyed the voluminous bag. "We should probably run by my loft on the way to the restaurant." At her curious glance he explained, "So I can change into something more suitable."

Her blue eyes slowly moved from the top of his black head down to his booted feet. "You're fine." Better than fine, she corrected mentally. The man's lean, hard body encouraged feminine fantasies that were anything but calming. Deciding that spending her time fantasizing about Darius Wilde's body would only get her into hot water, Sara returned her energy to locating her key.

"I know it's in here somewhere," she muttered, extracting a fat paperback novel, which she handed to Darius. A deck of cards, a two-headed gold coin, a chrome bicycle horn, three yellow tennis balls, assorted pencils—all with broken lead—three Snickers bars and a hairbrush followed.

Not for the first time, certainly, Sara wished that the organization she demonstrated in managing the Peter and Wendy Family Circus and Penguin Extravaganza would extend into her personal life. Sara knew that her

father could, upon request, locate a needle he'd se-
creted in a haystack three years earlier. As could her
mother and her brother. Sara, on the other hand, was
quite accustomed to walking around blind for an hour
every morning before stumbling across her contacts,
soaking wherever she'd left them the night before.

"There you are," Sara exclaimed happily when she
unearthed a gold wristwatch, a birthday present from
her mother, which she'd given up for lost. Sara had been
dreading having to admit she had misplaced the watch
once again.

"Nice watch," Darius said. "But how's it going to get
us into the house?"

"Oh, it isn't," Sara admitted with a quick grin. "But
you've no idea how worried I've been about losing it.
The last time I had lunch with my mother, I told her that
it was at the jeweler's for repairs, but unfortunately I've
never been a very convincing liar, so I'm almost certain she suspects the worst." Although Sara didn't consider herself any more superstitious than the next
person, she allowed herself to believe that finding the
watch was a good omen.

"Bingo!"

Her fingers closed around her brass house key.
Gathering her possessions from Darius's outstretched
hands, she dropped them back into the voluminous bag
and unlocked the door.

"I like your house," Darius said as she led him into a
room that for some incomprehensible reason reminded him of autumn in upstate New York.

"Thanks. You're welcome to fix yourself a drink while I change," she offered. "I think my brother left a bottle of Scotch in that bookcase next to the fireplace the last time he was down from New York. And there's some uncorked wine in the refrigerator from a party I had a while back."

The contents of her handbag had given Darius yet another insight into what he was fast deciding was a very complex personality. "How long ago was the party?"

Yanking the heavy wig off with a deep, heartfelt sigh of relief, she tossed it onto a nearby Regency chair. "New Year's Eve, I think."

Four and a half months earlier. Not entirely impossible if it was a red, he decided, remembering times when he'd drunk a lot worse.

Sara released her hair from the elastic band. Rippling waves of red-gold silk drifted enticingly over her shoulders. "No," she said reflectively, "that can't be right; I was in Vermont over New Year's."

"Christmas?" he suggested hopefully.

She shook her head. "Uh-uh. I was in London with my uncle; he's always insisted that England is the only place to be at Christmas." At his curious look Sara elaborated. "You know—Dickens, wassail bowls, plum pudding and all that."

"Of course."

Sara chewed thoughtfully on her thumbnail. "*Oktoberfest*," she finally replied. "I remember now because Mary Faller's husband, Werner, insisted that German wine was the only thing to serve with the sauerkraut and sausages. I think the last bottle is about a quarter full."

Darius had dined on sun-dried rhino meat on the Serengeti; he had existed for forty-five days on *tsampa*—a malodorous Tibetan staple consisting of barley flour, yak butter and tea—and sampled rancid seal flippers wrapped in blubber in the Far North. But he drew the line at drinking a wine that had been hanging around uncorked for seven and a half months.

"Thanks, anyway, but I think I'll wait for dinner."

"Suit yourself. I'll be back in a jiffy; feel free to look around if you'd like." She disappeared into an adjoining room.

The door hadn't quite clicked shut, and as his gaze drifted in that direction, Darius saw her reach up and pull the bulky dress over her head. Before he could turn away, she'd released the Velcro fasteners on the padding. Who would have imagined that under all that material she would be wearing a midnight-blue teddy with lace so fine it could have been spun from cobwebs?

Her body was slender, firm and, Darius imagined, even softer than the blue silk. Unaware of his scrutiny, Sara sighed and rubbed the back of her neck. When the gesture pulled the dark lace more tightly over her breasts, Darius felt an almost desperate need to touch her. Hold her. Unnerved by his uncharacteristic lack of self-control, he turned away, even as a dark corner of his masculine mind longed to see more.

This was ridiculous. He was behaving like a twelve-year-old boy drooling over his first glimpse of a *Play-*

boy magazine. Every cell in his body was suddenly on red alert, and he found himself wanting a cigarette when he hadn't smoked in seven years.

Get hold of yourself, Wilde, he castigated himself. *Which is stronger—the nicotine or you?* The ploy worked, as it always had. Darius could feel the need drifting away, like smoke on the wind.

All right, he decided, *let's try something a little more difficult. Which is stronger—your desire to taste that creamy skin at the back of her knees? Or you?* When his body stirred at the memory of those long, slender legs, Darius knew he had met his match. In order to direct his mutinous mind to a safer subject, Darius turned his attention to Sara's house.

As his gaze swept the room, he thought he could detect the aura of money. Old money, and lots of it. There was an air of effortless elegance in the decorating that instantly conveyed integrity and background, a feeling of roots.

A framed photograph on a nearby table caught his eye. A young girl—obviously Sara—was seated on the lap of a dark-haired man whose features were vaguely familiar. The man was soberly dressed in a double-breasted charcoal-gray suit; the child wore a pink velvet dress, lacy white stockings and black patent shoes. The gleaming clouds of Sara's hair had been tied back with a matching velvet ribbon, but several unruly strands had managed to escape, framing her face with soft, gently curling red-gold tendrils.

Although the photo had been formally posed, it would have been impossible to miss the impish gleam in the child's wide, blue eyes. Darius suspected that it had taken a vast amount of coaxing, along with an equal number of threats, to convince Sara to sit still for the few seconds it took to snap the photograph. When he looked back at the man's face, he noticed an identical devilish spark. That they were kindred spirits was more than evident; that they adored each other was also obvious.

"This man in the picture," he called out. "Is he your father?"

"My uncle." Her voice was muffled by the shower she had just turned on. "Actually, you might know him; he's lectured on ethics at the university."

Darius leaned closer, forcing himself to concentrate on the man rather than the child. Comprehension dawned. "Your uncle is Judge Walter Cornell?"

Recently retired from the federal bench, the man was considered by legal experts to be one of the premier jurists in the country. Darius had spoken with him briefly at various university social functions and had been surprised and pleased to learn that the judge had actually read his books.

"That's him," she agreed cheerfully. "Actually he's my uncle and best friend, along with Germaine, of course. Fortunately, when they coined the phrase sober as a judge, they weren't referring to Uncle Walter. He's the only member of the Cornell clan, with the possible exception of my older brother, Lincoln, who's ever understood my unorthodox streak."

A man who'd insist on celebrating Christmas in Dickens's homeland could probably relate to a Society Hill niece turned clown, Darius decided.

Sara McBride's character was turning out to be layers upon layers upon more enticing layers. The idea of spending the next three and a half months peeling them away, one at a time, was becoming more attractive by the moment.

Searching for additional clues to her personality, Darius continued his careful study of her living room. A pair of lemon-yellow shoes with ridiculously high heels rested haphazardly on a carpet he knew to be an Aubusson, while a half-finished jigsaw puzzle depicting the New York skyline at night claimed the tilt top of a Hepplewhite table.

"You didn't decorate this place yourself, did you?" he called out when he heard her turn off the water.

"No, I didn't. It was my mother's idea of a surprise housewarming gift when I moved in." From behind the partially closed door there was the enticing, unmistakable movement of Sara as she dressed. Once again his body stirred. Once again Darius gritted his teeth as he forced himself to ignore it. "I think she was afraid I'd be perfectly content living out of cardboard boxes and sleeping on the floor. Which, of course, is probably true. How did you know?"

He picked up a crystal ball on a nearby table and shook it, causing flakes of "snow" to fall onto a miniature Swiss village. "Just a hunch."

His interest piqued by the unexpected touch of whimsy in such a formally decorated room, Darius searched for more and found them. Buttery daffodils added a yellow glow to an intricately cut Waterford crystal vase. A Chinese bowl filled with a dark, spicy potpourri explained his initial memory of fall gardens. A colorful abstract in yellows and reds, obviously Sara's work, hung on a nearby wall.

A wooden nutcracker boasting a high plumed black hat and a wooden rifle draped over a bright red tunic stood eternal guard on one of the bookcase shelves, and nearby a brown bear sporting a ruffled pink tutu topped a glass music box. When he twisted the key, the bear began pirouetting in endless circles to Tchaikovsky's "Waltz of the Flowers."

"Do you live alone?" Darius asked.

"Yes."

"Who takes care of this place when you're out of town?" was his next question.

Sara laughed. "Now you sound just like my mother. She insists on her housekeeper coming by once a week to, quote, spruce things up, unquote. If you want my opinion, I think she lives in fear that my dust bunnies will begin multiplying and take over the world. Or at least Philadelphia. Which, of course, to my mother is the only part of the world that really matters."

Sara reentered the room. "I could definitely eat a horse." She'd changed into a pair of navy slacks and a silk blouse the color of poppies. The top two buttons of the blouse were undone, revealing a tantalizing V of flesh.

Although he'd already seen her almost nude, Darius was struck by how small she was. How delicate. Her wide blue eyes dominated her face, reminding him of the sky over Arizona. He'd like to take her to Arizona, Darius realized with a jolt. To share with her the wide open country where he had grown up.

He'd show her how the mountains, silhouetted against the sky, seemed to increase in size at sunset, take her sailing on tree-rimmed lakes, lie with her in a bed of fragrant wildflowers under a wide, cloudless sky. Touch her. Taste her.

"Darius?"

Her soft voice shattered his sensual daydream. As he jerked his thoughts back to the present, Darius realized she had asked him a question.

"Sorry. I was thinking about your eyes," he said with a quiet honesty that surprised them both.

"My eyes?"

"They're very beautiful."

A simple compliment, simply spoken, and certainly one she had heard before. But instinct told her that Darius Wilde was not a man to hand out pretty phrases very often. "Thank you."

He decided that he liked the way soft color drifted into her cheeks when she was pleased. "You're welcome."

Their gazes met and held and there was an instant of heat. For that fleeting second time seemed to freeze, and Sara had the uncanny feeling that she'd known this man all her life.

Darius was no less shaken as he felt their souls touch with a force that threatened to tilt the earth on its axis.

"You said something about a horse," he recalled after what seemed an eternity.

Still shaken, Sara forced her mind back to their conversation. "I said something about eating," she acknowledged. "And if we don't leave right now, I'll probably faint dead away before I make it to the restaurant."

"I think I like the idea of you swooning at my feet," he decided as they left the house.

Sara shot him a pointed look. "Don't hold your breath," she advised.

Ten minutes later they'd reached their destination, Sara maneuvering the car into a narrow parking space as if it had been designed with the hatchback in mind.

They were walking toward the restaurant when, without warning, Darius pulled her into a nearby doorway. "Come here for a minute," he said.

Sara was too stunned to protest as he drew her into his arms and without a moment's hesitation lowered his mouth, his lips brushing hers with a feather-soft touch that belied the hunger surging through his veins. It was more temptation than a proper kiss, more promise than pressure. As a rich, liquefying pleasure began to flow through her, Sara let out a shuddering little breath.

It was she who altered the angle, tilting her head to allow him to increase the pressure of the kiss. But Darius appeared content to let his lips drift gently over hers in a slow, lazy seduction that was as enticing as it was enervating. When he brushed her tingling skin with the tip of his tongue, she trembled. When he caught her lower lip lightly between his teeth and tugged, Sara's legs went numb. In sudden need of support, she curved her fingers around the top of his arms.

They were strong, she noted through the smoky haze clouding her mind. His muscles were firm, well defined, creating an image that contrasted with the stereotype of an individual who spent long solitary hours among dusty academic tomes. In a distant corner of her whirling mind Sara admitted that Darius Wilde was turning out to be a paradox even as she tried to forget that puzzles—all kinds—had always fascinated her.

As his clever, teasing lips drew her deeper and deeper into the swirling mists, Sara didn't realize that she had done anything to encourage him to deepen the kiss until she felt her fingers clasped around the nape of his neck. She went up on her toes, her body straining anxiously, hungrily against him.

Needs. They surged through him, beating away at his self-control, demanding satisfaction. In response to her unspoken plea his arms tightened, crushing her against him as his lips turned hard. Greedy. Darius's heated blood was pounding in his ears, and he no longer knew if the out-of-control heartbeat he felt thudding against his chest belonged to him or to her.

The distant sound of a trolley drifted on the night air; neither heard it. A fire engine careered around the nearby corner of 4th and South Streets, siren blaring, lights flashing; caught up in an exquisite conflagration of their own, Darius and Sara ignored it.

Desire, deeper and more complex than anything he had ever experienced, battered away at his insides. As his hands roamed up and down her back, Darius was stunned to realize that they were no longer steady. He had wanted women before. Other women had made him burn. But no woman had ever made him tremble.

Some deep-seated primitive instinct warned him that if he didn't back away now, it would be too late to prevent an emotional involvement. With an effort he broke the heated contact, although he couldn't resist burying his lips in the fragrant clouds of her hair. Somewhere nearby, the hooves of a mounted police horse clip-clopped in the night.

"I've been wanting to do that for hours."

Sara tilted her head back to look up at him. "Hours?"

"Ever since I saw you cry after leaving Mandy Johnson's room."

That he could remember one child's name out of the many he'd seen for the first time that day was yet another indication that she wasn't dealing with an ordinary man. "I wasn't crying."

Unable to resist touching her, he skimmed the back of his hand down the side of her face. "You were crying," he corrected softly. "And for good reason."

Sara expelled a slow, weary breath. "Mandy wants to be a ballerina when she grows up. That's all she can think about. It's what keeps her going. But if they can't find a kidney donor—" Her voice broke off. When her eyes filled with telltale moisture, she turned away, blinking furiously. "I'm sorry. I rarely cry. Really, I don't."

The small, grieving woman was a dramatic contrast to the dynamo he'd watched whirling her way through the hospital. She was also worlds away from the disorganized nymph who had invited him into her home. Darius found himself unreasonably attracted to all three of them.

He placed a kiss on the fiery crown of her head. "Hey, you're entitled," he said quietly. "Sometimes we all need to cry, Sara. It's part of the human condition." His fingers cupped her chin, tilting her head back for a quick, hard kiss.

It was going to be all right, Darius decided as they continued walking. Perhaps it had only been her weakened state, brought about by fatigue, anxiety and a lack of food, but she'd allowed him to slip around emotional barricades that he had been surprised to discover lurking behind such a carefree exterior. Barriers, he suspected, that had been a long time in the making.

Oh, it wasn't going to be easy. But they were going to spend the next sixteen weeks together. Of that much he was certain. And Darius had already decided, sometime between the daffodils and the dancing bear, that he was going to make love to Sara McBride.

4

THE SANDWICH SHOP WAS a rich concoction of scents: garlic, pastrami, yeast, freshly baked bread, espresso. Darius supposed that it had an Art Deco kind of charm, with its black-and-white tile and chrome interior. But most of the ground floor was taken up by service areas and ovens, and the one counter with bar stools along the opposite wall didn't lend itself to what he had hoped would be an intimate, getting-acquainted dinner.

"Jim's has the very best hoagies in the city," Sara assured him as she noticed his slight frown.

"I've always thought so myself, but I hadn't realized that we were having hoagies for dinner."

"You don't like hoagies?" Her incredulous tone suggested that he might as well denigrate the flag, motherhood and apple pie while he was at it.

"Since we'd already determined that I was paying, I'd planned to have a steak."

"No problem; you can have a steak submarine. It's enormous, and smothered with melted cheese. It even won an award in *Philadelphia* magazine," she said coaxingly when he continued to frown. "You'll love it."

Her smile was what did it. It was warm and golden, like summer sunlight. "I'm sure I will," he agreed.

They placed their order—one hoagie, one steak sandwich, root beer for her, two bottles of Dock Street beer for him. Darius watched with undisguised awe as Sara's sandwich was created. Sliced layers of salami, provolone and prosciutto were laid atop the open faces of an enormous sliced Italian roll and drenched in olive oil and vinegar. After that came lettuce, tomatoes, green peppers, onions and hot peppers, with more olive oil at the end.

"There's certainly nothing subtle about your gastronomic taste," he murmured as he watched the counter man wrap the Herculean sandwich. "Or your appetite."

"I told you I was starving," she reminded him as she gathered a handful of paper napkins.

"I'll say this for you," he said, paying for their dinner with a ten-dollar bill and pocketing the change, "you're a cheap date."

"This isn't a date," Sara insisted. "It's merely a business dinner. To set ground rules for the upcoming tour."

"Thanks for reminding me; I'll make a note to claim it on my income-tax return," he said as they returned to the car. "Where to now?"

"I thought we might take them back to my place."

"Uh-uh," Darius decided suddenly. "I'd rather go to mine."

"Why?"

"I want to show you something."

She raised a coppery brow. "Etchings?"

"Better," he assured her with quiet amusement.

He gave her the address, and although Sara drove
with her usual disregard for speed limits, the trip from
the restaurant to Darius's loft seemed to take an eternity. She'd never noticed before how cramped the
cockpit-like interior of the hatchback actually was;
Darius Wilde seemed to fill the small space with his
presence. Unnerved by the silence between them, she
reached out and turned on the radio.

It had to be prophetic, she decided, as the radio, set
to her favorite jazz station, began playing a female vo-
calist singing "I Got It Bad and That Ain't Good," with
Duke Ellington's orchestra. *You and me, both, Ivie,
baby,* Sara considered wryly.

"Ivie Anderson," Darius murmured appreciatively.
"She's always been one of my favorites."

Sara glanced over at him in surprise. "She's not very
well known."

"Not as well known as Billie Holiday or Dinah
Washington," he acknowledged. "But she should have
been a major star. Ivie could suggest more in a single
phrase than a lot of singers could in several choruses."

Sara nodded her agreement, even as she allowed
herself to ponder the chances of meeting a man who not
only appreciated jazz, but also shared her taste. She was
well aware that the quickest way to start an argument
among jazz aficionados was to ask them to make up a
list of certified jazz singers. Yet if his comments concerning Ivie Anderson were any indication, she and
Darius agreed on at least one.

She was strongly tempted to test the phenomena a bit
further when a small, self-protective instinct that sur-

faced from time to time pointed out that Darius Wilde was too arrogant. Too intriguing. And most of all, the man was too damn sexy. Sara couldn't help wondering if this time she might have bitten off more than she could chew.

She was surprised to find that Darius's loft was located in Manayunk, an ethnic neighborhood that had once been described as the Manchester of America. "I would have expected you to live in University City."

"It'd be more convenient," he agreed, "but it's become a bit too yuppified in the past few years for my taste."

Realizing that she'd just accidentally stumbled across yet another thing they had in common, Sara's gaze swept the darkened street. "Well, you certainly can't complain about that here."

"Yet," he qualified. "You know, I moved here for the village atmosphere of the neighborhood—its long-term stability—but in doing so, I'm contributing to the eventual extinction of everything I love about the place. As an anthropologist, I should know enough to leave it alone; as a distinctly flawed human, I'm willing to put my own needs and desires above that of the group."

"But if you didn't move here, someone else would."

He smiled slightly. "That's the same rationalization I use every day."

"Does it work?"

His smile deepened. "Sometimes."

If she was at all surprised by Darius Wilde's neighborhood, Sara found the interior of his airy, spacious loft a revelation.

"I don't believe this," she breathed, looking around the high white walls covered with circus posters. Her gaze settled momentarily on a brightly colored Stafford poster depicting an equestrienne jumping through a paper balloon, circa 1890. "These are incredible."

"I thought you might like them."

"Like them?" Sara laughed as she stopped in front of a poster for a Danish Wild West show. "I adore them. Who wouldn't?"

A framed newspaper advertisement for John Bill Rickett's first circus in Philadelphia, 1793, shared the wall with a Russian poster for the Sobolyevkiye Riding Act, a premier *voltige* troupe. As could be expected, there were a number of Ringling Brothers and Barnum and Bailey posters, all lavishly printed, magnificently designed.

She couldn't resist a small burst of pride when she saw a Peter and Wendy Family Circus and Penguin Extravaganza poster in bright primary colors of yellow, red and blue. Not having the funds available to hire commercial artists, Sara had designed that particular poster herself and was inordinately proud of it.

"Oh, my God, you have a poster of Helga," she exclaimed, her eyes brightening as she drank in a dazzling poster depicting an impossibly beautiful trapeze artist. "She'd be absolutely ecstatic."

"Helga?"

"She used to be an aerialist for the Circus Knie in Switzerland," Sara explained. "Then one day while on tour she met Yuri Pavlovich, a clown and wire walker for a Russian circus, in a Rome train depot. Although they were headed in opposite directions, the trains, not surprisingly, were late. It took two hours for them to fall in love, three months for Yuri to defect and another five years for them to make it to the United States. They've been with the Peter and Wendy Family Circus and Penguin Extravaganza from the start."

Her smile was quick. "You'll love them; she's a restrained perfectionist, with every blond hair in place, even when she's hanging by her heels from the trapeze. Yuri is amazingly disorganized, emotional and tends toward long, passionate discourses on everything from the sorry state of America's infrastructure to the genius of Billy Joel."

"Sounds like a match made in heaven." Darius put the bags of food down on a table. "Do you realize that was the first time you brought up my traveling with the circus without looking as if you'd been sentenced to a summer of hard labor?"

Uncomfortable with holding in her emotions, Sara went up on her toes and touched her lips lightly to his cheek. "That was before I knew about the posters."

Darius smiled as he brushed away a cloud of hair that had drifted over her eyes. "And here I thought it was because you couldn't resist my kisses."

Her eyes warmed at the memory, but Darius thought he detected a touch of wariness in their clear blue depths as well. "You kiss very well," she agreed politely. "But it was the posters that did it."

She moved across the room to a bookcase. As she scanned the spines, she noticed that his taste in literature was as eclectic as his decorating. *Anna Karenina* shared shelf space with *House of the Seven Gables*; nearby she spotted a biography of H. L. Mencken by William Manchester and a *Peanuts Treasury*. As her study continued, Sara saw a thick, all-too-familiar book that made her groan out loud.

"Oh, no, you're Dr. D. J. Wilde," she moaned, wondering how the name could have possibly escaped her.

"That's me," he agreed. "But you already knew that."

"I knew your name. But for some reason it didn't ring a bell. I didn't realize who you were. I mean, who you are. It never even crossed my mind that Germaine's Darius Wilde was *the* Dr. D. J. Wilde. Oh, dear, and here I was, having the nerve to question you about why any publisher would be willing to buy your book on the strength of a synopsis. You must think that I'm an absolute idiot!"

Darius raised an amused brow. "I suppose there's a modicum of logic hiding somewhere in that charmingly convoluted statement."

"I read *Drumbeats* last month. Three times."

His expression was one of uncensored pleasure. "You enjoyed it that much?"

"I loved it. The first time I'd only planned on skimming a few of the shorter tales before going to bed."

"Tell me that you were hooked and I'll be your willing slave for life."

"The next thing I knew it was morning. I'd sat up reading all night. The second time I was playing *Graceland* in the background on my CD. The stories seemed to come alive even more."

"Perhaps I should assign Paul Simon a percentage of my royalties."

Sara shook her head. "Oh, no, you're definitely entitled to them; it was a powerful piece of work, Darius. Insightful, intelligent, warm, but decidedly unsettling. A few of the stories left me feeling horribly uncomfortable. And sad. Would you think me a silly, overly emotional woman if I told you that I cried? Each and every time?"

She could not have said anything that would have pleased him more. *Drumbeats* had been unanimously well reviewed; even some talk-show hosts had expressed their appreciation of the native South African folktales. But Darius couldn't recall anyone's opinion meaning more to him than Sara's did at this moment.

"Thank you."

Once again his words were so simply stated. If her former husband had received the accolades Darius Wilde had received during his career, he would have been impossible to live with. Not that he hadn't been, anyway.

"You're not at all what I expected," she murmured, turning away from those steady dark eyes as she pretended to examine a Maori warrior mask.

Darius crossed the room to her. Although Sara hadn't turned around, she suddenly realized that he was very, very close.

Her hair, illuminated by the soft track lighting, appeared to gleam. What would it look like in the iridescent light of early morning? he wondered. Spread across his pillow, with the glow of sunrise streaking in through the high eastern windows. He had an almost overwhelming need to know.

"And what, exactly, were you expecting?"

His voice was deep, velvety, and all too enticing. Sara knew that were she to turn around, she would find the dark desire in his eyes almost impossible to resist. "A stuffy academic, I suppose." Willpower kept her voice steady as his hands settled on her shoulders. Underneath the poppy silk her skin came alive. "Arrogant. Insufferable."

Darius hadn't missed her slight tremor. "Pompous," he supplied. "Filled with myself."

"Exactly." She was a grown woman, long past the age of infatuation. So why was it this man could make her so breathless with such a light, unthreatening touch?

"Interested solely in my career." His hands lifted the fiery clouds of hair, allowing his lips access to the nape of her neck. "My desires. My needs."

Sara was not an inexperienced woman. But she had never felt anything to equal the way Darius Wilde could make her feel with a single touch. A single look.

She turned, lifting slender hands that were none too steady to his shoulders. It was all she could do to keep her fingers from exploring the hard ridge of muscle she felt under the faded chambray. "Really, Darius," she said in a rushed, shaky voice that revealed her discomfort with the situation, "you did promise to feed me. I could certainly do with my sandwich right about now. How about you?"

Her eyes, although she was struggling valiantly to hide it, were wide blue pools of need. Her light scent surrounded them while her delicate, unpainted mouth tempted, enticed.

"Later."

His head lowered and even as she knew she was playing with fire, Sara's lips parted in warm, accepting anticipation. But she was soon to discover that nothing about Darius was at all predictable. His lips barely skimmed the corner of her mouth before moving along her jaw.

"So soft," he murmured. "And sweet."

Desire rippled just under her skin. Sara tilted her head, but Darius easily evaded her silent plea. "You're not at all what I expected, either," he murmured as his lips glided along the narrow, upswept line of her cheekbones.

"I'm not?" Sara drew in a quick breath when his teeth tugged lightly at her earlobe.

"Not at all. You're a great deal more lovely." Darius soothed the tender skin with the tip of his tongue, leaving sparks where his teeth had played. "More passionate."

When those teasing, tormenting lips slid over her temple, Sara's blood seemed to leap in response. "Darius..."

Her breath was warm against his skin, her slender body was trembling in his arms like a strong but supple willow in the wind. He could have her now, Darius knew. He could drag her down to the dhurrie rug without her uttering a single word of protest. Or he could lift her into his arms and carry her to his wide bed where they would spend the rest of a long and passion-filled night making love in myriad ways and moods until the sun rose and it was time for them to leave.

The idea was as exciting as it was alluring. But even as he felt his body hardening, responding to her feverish need, Darius knew that one night with the luscious Sara McBride would not be enough. He wanted... what? Darius asked himself as a soft little moan escaped Sara's parted lips. More, he realized on an almost blinding flash. He wanted a great deal more than a single passion-filled night.

Her blood was beating so fiercely in her head that Sara could hardly think straight. All she knew was that once again this man had led her to the very brink of insanity. And once again she'd gone all too willingly.

"I think that was a bad idea." She dropped her hands and moved away.

"Not bad. Perhaps premature," he allowed. "But what we experienced at the restaurant, and just now, was a long, long way from bad, Sara." He draped a friendly arm around her shoulders and led her to a sofa covered with a Navaho blanket woven in subtle earth tones reminiscent of Arizona's Monument Valley.

"It was reckless."

"I find it difficult to believe that you've never been reckless."

Sara sighed. "If you asked my family, they'd undoubtedly tell you that reckless is my middle name."

"It sounds as if you disagree."

"I'll admit to being impulsive, but reckless..." She shook her head. "I don't think so." *Not until now*, she added silently. *Until you.*

"I suppose this is where I should assure you that I'll be on my best behavior while accompanying you on the tour," Darius said as he handed her her sandwich.

Sara wondered why she found that idea vaguely disappointing. Impulsive she might be, but she certainly wasn't foolish enough to get emotionally involved with this man. "That would ease my mind considerably."

"I'm afraid I'm going to have to let you down," he said as he sat down beside her on the comfortable sofa.

She looked up at him, studying his casually friendly expression with a great deal more care. "What's that supposed to mean?"

His thumb brushed up her cheek in a long, sweeping arc. "We are going to make love, Sara," he assured her gravely. When she opened her mouth to object, his mood changed like lightning and he shot her a bold, self-assured grin that should have infuriated her, but for some unfathomable reason didn't. "But I'm willing to let you get used to the idea."

She glared at him, struggling not to succumb to the devilish gleam in his eyes. The dancing, rebellious light reminded her of her uncle. Darius Wilde had a great deal in common with Judge Walter Cornell, Sara decided. Both were extremely intelligent men, highly respected in their professions. And both were all too accustomed to getting their own way.

"You know, of course, that you're insufferable," she said calmly.

Darius's response was a cheerful, unrepentant grin that would have done justice to Huck Finn. "So I've been told."

As they ate supper, they kept the conversation on neutral ground, discussing such things as the Phillies' chances for the World Series that year, the 76ers and, always a safe topic, the weather.

"By the way," Darius said, "I forgot to ask you, how did your parents like their Sara McBride seascape?"

"Oh, that." Sara frowned as she recalled her parents' reaction to her painting. "My father professed to like it, but since *unusual* is not a word he normally uses to denote extreme pleasure, I have a feeling he would have preferred a tie."

"How about your mother?" Darius couldn't imagine any mother not appreciating any gift her child had made. His mother continued to treasure the clay ashtray he'd made in the third grade. She kept paper clips and safety pins in it.

Sara shrugged. "Mother said something vague about the bedroom drapes and the wallpaper and blue being a difficult color to match." She forced a grin. "Perhaps you're going to be stuck with it after all, Darius."

She was hurt. That much was obvious. He wanted to do something—anything—to make it better. "Sara—"

The conversation had suddenly gotten too personal. Sara looked down at her watch. "My goodness, I had no idea that it was so late. I'd better be going," she said, rising.

Although frustrated, Darius decided he had no choice but to let her leave. "What time do we hit the road?"

"What would you say if I told you six-thirty? In the morning," she added, with a warning look.

"I'd suggest you conserve valuable time by spending the night here."

His mild tone made her laugh. "Don't you ever give up?"

As his body responded instinctively to the provocative, silvery sound of her laughter, Darius slipped his hands into his back pockets to keep from touching her. "No. Not when I want something—someone—badly enough."

Sara tilted her head to one side, studying him soberly. "You make me sound like just another possession you want to acquire," she murmured. "Along the lines of a pre-Columbian dagger. Or a Jamaican voodoo charm."

He gave her a long patient look. "I think you know better than that, Sara."

"Do I?" She ran her hand through her hair, struggling for composure but horribly afraid she was losing the battle. "I suppose that's something I'm going to have to think about."

"You do that," he agreed amiably. "And while you're thinking about it, consider the fact that your skin flames when I touch you here." He ran his fingers along her collarbone. He nodded, satisfied, when he felt her pulse beat rapidly at the base of her throat. "And here." His fingers inched slowly downward.

"Darius..."

"Here." His intimate touch was unmistakably possessive. "Think about it, Sara. When you're lying awake tonight, wishing that you'd given in to impulse and spent the night with me. In my bed. Where you belong."

"I'm agreeing to your accompanying the circus for two reasons," she said with a great deal more equanimity than she was feeling.

"And those are?"

"Number one, my affection for Germaine. She's a good friend; there isn't anything I wouldn't do for her."

He nodded. "My feelings exactly. And reason number two?"

"You're an excellent writer; and although I still can't understand why a renowned anthropologist would be interested in documenting a small traveling circus, I trust you to be fair."

"Thank you. Why do I get the impression that compliment is only a prelude to the insult yet to come?"

Once again Sara reminded herself that Darius was an intensely perceptive man. She would be well advised, over the coming months, to keep that fact in mind.

"It's not an insult," she insisted. "Merely a suggestion for making things run smoother."

He folded his arms across his chest. "Smoother."

Sara bobbed her head, causing a few curls to fall over her forehead. "That's right," she said, blowing them away. "I'll admit that I'm attracted to you, Darius. Although I doubt that should come as any surprise; after all, women all over the world have probably tumbled willingly into your bed. My goodness, when you think of all the places Dr. D. J. Wilde has traveled, the possibilities just boggle the mind. Why, you've probably made love to women from Fairbanks to Fresno to Fuji and all points in between. I'll bet all you ever have to do is crook that little finger and—"

"Sara," Darius interrupted patiently, "do you think we could skip the details of my exaggerated and highly fictional worldwide harem and get to the part where you suggest that we establish a rule that forbids mixing work with pleasure for the next three and a half months?"

Her face settled into stubborn lines. "I really believe it would be best." Sara wondered exactly who she was trying harder to convince—Darius or herself.

"Since we both have a busy day ahead of us in only a few hours, I'll decline to argue that point," he said with a nonchalance that didn't fool Sara for a moment. This was not a man to give up without a fight. Of that she was certain.

"Thank you," she said as he accompanied her down to the street in the slow, creaky freight elevator. "I really believe, when you've given it some thought, Darius, that you'll agree with me."

Her intense expression was at such odds with what Darius knew to be the softness of her lips that he had to fight back a grin as they walked toward her car. Although he was relieved to see that all four tires were still intact, it crossed his mind that if one of his more larcenous neighbors had only seen fit to "borrow" them, she'd have yet another excuse to give in to temptation and spend the night with him.

"May I give you a piece of advice?" he asked as she slid into the driver's seat.

Her eyes, as she looked up at him, were unmistakably wary. "I suppose so."

"The best thing about rules, sweetheart, is that they're made to be broken." He cupped her chin with his hand and pressed a quick, hard kiss against her mouth, then closed the car door after her. He paused before turning away and said, "Oh, and Sara?"

She was sitting there, her fingers pressed against her lips, as if she could still feel the lingering heat. "Yes?"

Darius gave her a slow, wickedly insinuating wink. "Sweet dreams."

Standing alone on the curb, he watched until the amber taillights of her car disappeared around the corner. Then, with his hands shoved deep into the pockets of his jeans, Darius returned to his loft, whistling a happy, off-key version of Grover Washington, Jr.'s "Come Morning."

5

ANTICIPATION ALONG WITH unbidden, erotic thoughts of Darius Wilde kept Sara tossing and turning until her alarm clock shattered the silence of the predawn darkness.

She crawled from her bed with a deep, heartfelt groan, managing to shower, brush her teeth and dress while in a dull, zombie-like state. At the best of times, Sara was not a morning person; after a short, sleepless night she harbored serious doubts that she would ever feel human again. It took several strong cups of coffee, but by the time she arrived at the circus grounds, she had begun to feel that she just might live.

The crew had struck the show last night; several tons of equipment, costumes and props had been packed into a large truck and six small red-and-white circus wagons, which would be transported on a flatbed trailer. The vans and motor homes that the troupe would call home for the next three months would lead the way during the trek. Yet another wagon, which opened up into a bandstand complete with an antique calliope that Sara had been thrilled to find at an auction in Atlantic City last winter, would bring up the rear of the procession.

The cool morning air was rife with excitement as the performers milled around, laughing, joking, relating anecdotes of previous tours for the newcomers.

If it was true that touring was exhausting, expensive and often tedious, Sara knew that it was also true that travel was part of the mystique of circuses. By its very nature, the circus was rooted in rootlessness; certainly no one had ever run away to the circus to stay at home.

As she walked across the open field, the pearly light of dawn was shimmering on the horizon, giving the scene an almost surrealistic quality. Spotting a small cluster of children near a blue van emblazoned with red and yellow stars, she strolled over, knowing ahead of time what she'd find.

Yuri Pavlovich was standing on an overturned box, surrounded by a group of wide-eyed children. Sara tried to remember a single time in the six years she'd known the Russian clown that she'd seen him without an attentive audience of children, and came up blank.

"Imagination," the diminutive performer announced, "is the most important aspect of clowning."

"What if you don't have a 'magination?" one of the children asked.

Yuri pulled himself up to his full height of five feet four inches. "Don't be such a silly goose. Everyone has an imagination."

"Stephen doesn't," another voice piped up. A girl with fat yellow braids tied at the ends with pieces of red yarn pointed toward a boy on the fringes of the small semicircle. The small, dark-haired boy appeared to shrink in response to the number of eyes suddenly directed his way.

"Ah, Stiva, come here and we will show these doubting Thomasinas how wrong they are."

"Doubting Thomases." This came from one of the older girls. "Thomasina was a cat. I saw the movie last week on cable."

Yuri shrugged. "Thomas, Thomasina, what does it matter? The important thing is that we demonstrate our good friend Stiva's imagination."

The encouraging shouts of the other children were almost deafening. Sara decided that Yuri and Stephen needed a little help to get things rolling.

"Perhaps some makeup is in order." She pulled a small box from her denim tote bag and, using only a black grease pencil, managed to create with a few quick, deft strokes, a little tramp, reminiscent of Charlie Chaplin.

"See what you think," she suggested softly, handing the shy young boy a mirror.

It would have been impossible to miss the light in Stephen's grave, dark eyes as he viewed himself. Without hesitation he went forward to join Yuri atop the overturned box.

"Aha," Yuri exclaimed, staggering backward, clutching his heart in a pantomime of shock, "what have we here? A Sad Sack who has taken the place of our dear friend Stiva!" The Russian exchanged a quick, appreciative glance with Sara, who merely grinned and nodded.

"Nice trick," said a deep voice behind her.

Fighting down a bubbling burst of pleasure, Sara turned around. "Sometimes things are easier to do when you're pretending to be someone else."

It hadn't been his imagination after all, Darius decided as he looked down at Sara. She was every bit as beautiful as he had remembered, as she had appeared in his frustratingly erotic fantasies during the short, sleepless night. She hadn't wasted time on primping this morning—her creamy complexion was free of make-up, and her lush red-gold hair had been pulled back into a casual ponytail. Although she'd fixed her hair only a short time before, curly tendrils had already escaped the elastic band to frame her face.

She was every dream he'd ever had come true; it was all he could do not to reach out and touch that creamy, smiling face.

"Is that the reason for Sassy Sally?" he asked, genuinely curious. "Does she allow you to behave in ways that Sara Cornell McBride wouldn't dare to?"

The question was one she'd been asked hundreds of times before. Still, coming from him, it seemed intensely personal. Too personal.

"I suppose there's a part of me in Sally," she agreed mildly, returning her attention to Yuri, who was presently having Stephen imagine that someone had just smashed a raw egg on top of his head.

"He's good," Darius commented, watching the talented clown.

"Isn't he?" Sara agreed. "Sometimes I really envy him."

"Why? Surely you don't envy his talent; Sassy Sally is a delightful creation."

"She's entertaining, in a bombastic sort of way," Sara agreed thoughtfully. "But when I take off the makeup and the costume, I always seem to leave a vital part of her in the trunk. Yuri, on the other hand, is all of his characters; his performance consists of simply stopping to listen to the voices inside his head."

"We should all do more of that."

Sara shot him a brief, pleased look. "I've always thought so."

"Like now."

"Now?" Lifting her gaze, Sara met his. Desire, passion, need—they were all there. But there was something else in those gleaming depths as well. An emotion so strong, so vibrant that it almost took her breath away. If she hadn't known better, she'd have thought it was . . .

No, that miniscule bit of Cornell practicality that she was always surprised to find lurking deep inside her reprimanded her more imaginative side, it couldn't be love. It was lust. Chemistry. Nothing more.

Darius leaned toward her, resting one hand on the side of a large Ford truck bearing the name of the circus in bold red script. "Now," he agreed, running his knuckles gently up the side of her face. "Do you know how much every one of my inner voices is urging me to kiss you?"

The rising sun was splintering the sky with color, and in the branches of a nearby tree birds filled the soft air with their morning song. Usually such simple things brought Sara pleasure, but she was fast discovering that nothing could compete with the enticing feel of his fingers caressing her skin. She watched the need rising in his eyes, hot and unrestrained, and felt it echoed deep within her own warming body.

"I think I'd like that. A lot," she admitted.

"So would I. So why did I hear a *but* in your tone?"

She glanced around at the bustling scene. "I really don't think this is a good time, Darius."

He arched his left brow. "Don't tell me that you're honestly afraid that a simple kiss will blow your virtuous reputation with the other members of the Peter and Wendy Family Circus?"

"There's going to be enough speculation when I begin introducing you around; I wouldn't want everyone to think that we were . . ." Color suffused her cheeks. "You know."

"Lovers."

"Exactly."

"I think I envy him, too," he said quietly.

Sara's gaze followed his across the field. "Yuri? Why?"

"Do you know how long it's been since I relied solely on my instincts?" He traced his finger tantalizingly over her lips, remembering their taste, wanting more.

His tender touch was causing her muscles to go lax. "How could I know that?" she asked distractedly. "Since I don't even know you."

Through the soft fog clouding her mind, Sara half expected Darius to protest that she knew everything she needed to know. Like the fact that all he had to do was look at her in that desirous way to have her body aching for his touch. Or the way she'd spent a sleepless night, imagining his broad, dark hands on her body, unlocking hidden emotions even she didn't know she had.

Or that even now, knowing that such behavior could well be considered foolhardy, she wanted nothing more than to experience the overwhelming passion he could bring to a single kiss.

Instead, his expression turned thoughtful as he looked down into her faintly flushed face. He couldn't remember ever seeing anything that affected him more than the uncensored warmth in her wide blue eyes. Other women tended to be more circumspect, more likely to play the game by the time-honored rules. Sara, on the other hand, either couldn't be bothered, or had never learned those rules in the first place.

"No, you don't," Darius said slowly. His slow smile harbored no hint of frustration or irritation. "Well, if there's one thing we're going to have lots of, it's time to get to know each other."

Sara's answering grin was quick and unrestrained. And decidedly relieved. "That's what you think. You're going to be working so hard during the day that it'll be all you can do to strip off your clothes before you collapse at night. And then, just when you're into a deep, satisfying sleep, the alarm will go off and it'll be time to start all over again."

"Don't worry about me; writing gives me a natural high. I'll be in great shape at night." He gave her a friendly leer. "Able to handle any naughty little ideas you might come up with."

Sara's eyes were wide and as guileless as a kitten's. "Oh, dear. Didn't I tell you?"

"Tell me what?"

"Goodness, I must not have. How could such an important thing have slipped my mind?"

Darius's eyes narrowed. "Why don't you just fill me in now?" he suggested.

"You have to understand, Darius, that the Peter and Wendy Family Circus and Penguin Extravaganza is a great deal like an actual family. We eat together, sleep together, spend hours on the road together. We all share the work; we agreed in the beginning that there would be no artificial division of labor with low-paid roustabouts doing the dirty jobs so the stars can loll about and sign autographs. If someone doesn't fit into the system, that person simply has to go."

"Are you saying that I'm going to be part of the troupe?"

Sara nodded her head. "That's precisely what I'm saying."

"But I don't have any performing talents."

"Oh, everyone has some talent," she assured him. "But don't worry about a thing, Darius. You can work as a roustabout until we manage to uncover yours."

"This wasn't part of our deal."

"Our deal was that you join us on the tour; I believe I've already explained that we have one very basic, very simple rule."

He arched a brow challengingly. "And that is?"

She smiled sweetly. "He who doesn't work doesn't eat."

"What makes you think writing isn't work?"

Still smiling, she patted his arm. "I'm sure it is. But Germaine has already explained to me that you're a perfectionist, Darius. She assured me that you would insist on immersing yourself fully in this latest project."

"So, following that line of reasoning, if I agree to act as roustabout—"

"You'll understand ever so much more about what makes us tick," she agreed, laughing up at him.

Darius shrugged, knowing when he'd been outmaneuvered. "Lady," he said, "you've got yourself a deal. But only because I've been wanting to write this book for years."

Her eyes twinkled with a merry light. "We'll certainly try to live up to your expectations, although I still don't think we can prove nearly as intriguing as a group of Amazonian Indians."

He reached down and took her hand in his. Thrills skittered up her spine as he brushed his thumb lazily over her knuckles. "Why don't you let me be the judge of that," he suggested as soberly as his slow, wolfish grin would allow.

NEW HOPE, HONEY BROOK, Mount Joy. Sinking Spring. Bird in Hand. The names of small towns told their own stories as the troupe of traveling players moved across the state. They found a modern-day War of the Roses going on in the rolling fertile farmland outside Philadelphia: brilliant red roses bloomed on the Lancaster side of the bridge crossing the Susquehanna River; fragrant white roses had been planted on the York side.

Red Pennsylvania Dutch barns with colorful decorative motifs—starbursts, rosettes, wheels and whirligigs—brightened the countryside, the hexes designed, among other things, to keep the barns free of witches. Sara knew that they were also supposed to ensure a perfect marriage, industrious children, food for the family and rain for the crops.

"A prudent people, the Pennsylvania Dutch," Darius murmured, one afternoon. They had stopped for lunch in the shade of a barn decorated with an amazing number of the bright hex signs.

"I suppose you don't believe in hex signs," Sara said, fully expecting a long lecture on the folly of trusting in ancient myths and legends.

Darius looked up at a bright rosette designed to ward off disease and pestilence, studying it thoughtfully as he chewed a mouthful of his chicken sandwich. "I never disbelieve anything," he said finally. "I've seen too many things that defy rational explanation."

He grinned as he reached out and ruffled her hair in an easy, familiar gesture. "Besides, you have to admit you hardly ever hear of witches in a Pennsylvania Dutchman's barn."

Once again he had managed to surprise and please her. Sara smiled, content just to bask in his presence and the gentle spring day.

As they moved across the state, into Ohio, across Indiana and Illinois, they passed one small town after another where life seemed to have remained as quiet as a leaf changing color. Familiar sights became new; the ordinary was magically transformed into the sublime. Every few hours they would rejoin the main highway and enter a forest of commercial enterprises, souped-up strips emblazoned with neon that clashed with the environment. As she did every year, Sara found herself wishing that they could stick to the back roads, where the people, as well as the towns, seemed to have held on to their individuality.

If the first eight days of the season were any indication, Sara considered as she went over the receipts one evening, the circus might actually end the tour in the black. The gate receipts were up more than twenty percent from the previous year.

The Peter and Wendy Family Circus and Penguin Extravaganza was unique compared with the larger traveling circuses because it operated by performing benefit shows for nonprofit community organizations. The sponsoring group earned a dollar from each ticket sold, plus proceeds from the midway the group members were responsible for setting up outside the entrance to the circus tent. The proceeds from these performances accounted for approximately seventy-five percent of the troupe's expenses; the remaining twenty-five percent came in the form of grants from federal and local governments, corporations and philanthropic individuals.

Although none of the performers could ever be accused of getting rich—indeed, most of them were working at below minimum wage—there was a freedom of discovery and enthusiasm shared by the performers and the audience that made it all worthwhile most days.

The tour itself was admittedly grueling. And becoming more so every year as they added more and more stops in their trek across the country. Still, Sara thought, there was something to be said for spending the season living in tents with a group of talented individuals who in many ways continued to behave like children: it always reminded her of summer camp.

Her fears about Darius interfering with the day-to-day workings of the circus appeared to have been unfounded. Although the members of the troupe all liked him and appeared genuinely interested in his project, they were much too busy with their own creative activities to waste precious time and energy worrying about whether or not they'd show up in the pages of his finished book.

While she was relieved that Darius hadn't disrupted the workings of the circus, Sara was surprised and vaguely disappointed when, after the first morning, he continued to treat her no differently than any other member of the troupe. Although he was always cordial—even friendly—there was nothing to indicate that he had once vowed to make love to her.

In fact, she considered, thinking back on this evening, when Helga and Yuri had attempted to teach him to juggle with the Indian clubs to the vast amusement of the rest of the troupe, it was almost as if she'd imagined the passion that had sprung up between them.

She had just closed the bulky ledger when there was a slight movement outside the flap of her tent. Like many of the performers, Sara preferred the tent to either a van or a motor home.

"Come in," she called out, checking her reflection in a nearby mirror, just in case it was Darius.

"*Guten Abend,*" Helga Pavlovich greeted her. "You're working late."

"I was just going over the accounts."

"I will come back another time," the tall blond woman said immediately.

"Don't go." Sara shook her head as she gave her friend a crooked, sheepish grin. "I know I'm always a bear when I do the books, but I promise not to growl if you'll stay and have a cup of tea with me. We haven't had any time to talk—woman to woman—since we left Philadelphia."

"*Ja,* tea would be nice," Helga agreed. "And you are right, we should talk. Especially about your writer."

"He's not *my* writer," Sara corrected as she put a kettle on the burner of the portable camp stove and turned on the gas. "By the way, speaking of the accounts, our receipts so far are way over last year's."

"That's not surprising since all the performances have been sold out. And even if they don't continue to, since you had that *wunderbar* idea of making the groups put up a guarantee, we should not end up working for pennies. And of course he's *your* writer; you are, after all, the one who brought him here."

Although Sara and Helga had been close friends for years, Sara didn't want to talk about Darius. At least until she could understand her own mind. Her own heart. "My brother, Lincoln, had the *wunderbar* idea. He's the businessman in the family. I'm the clown."

Thoughtful lines marred the alabaster smoothness of Helga's brow. "I think sometimes you are too hard on yourself, Sara. You are a very capable person; surely your family realizes that what you've done with this circus in only five years is nothing short of remarkable."

The teakettle began to whistle. "My family's expertise is in law, banking and the stock market, in that order," Sara said as she poured water over a tea bag in a pot and left it to steep. "My parents have never been fans of the circus," she said quietly as she set out two earthenware mugs, one covered with balloons, the other boasting a trio of juggling clowns. "In fact, I'm convinced that my father considers us somewhere below actors and just above tap dancers in his sociological pecking order."

"Perhaps," Helga agreed reluctantly. She'd met the elder Cornell for the first time last year when he'd come backstage after a performance. That Sara's father had been uncomfortable surrounded by a tentful of clowns, jugglers and trapeze artists had been obvious. His conversation had been as stiff as his back. Even Helga, who was known for her restraint, had found the man unbearably stuffy. "But your brother has always proved very helpful."

"Linc's a good sport," Sara admitted.

"And your uncle not only approves of your life, it's also impossible to miss the fact that he is very, very proud of your accomplishments."

"Uncle Walter has always been known for his open mind. I suppose that's a necessity on the bench." She poured the tea, then handed Helga the cup with the clowns, keeping the balloon-festooned one for herself.

"I suppose so." Helga blew on the tea to cool it. "He's very handsome."

"I've always thought so. All that lush silver hair is a decided plus. Not to mention that he's in remarkable shape. Especially for a man approaching his sixty-seventh birthday."

"I was not speaking of your uncle."

"I know."

"He's also very intelligent."

"I also know that."

"And hardworking."

"Ditto."

"Nice."

"Agreed."

Helga sipped her tea, eyeing Sara over the rim of her mug. "And of course he's madly in love with you."

Sara coughed, spewing Earl Grey over her cotton shorts. "That's ridiculous," she complained, dabbing furiously at the drops of dark liquid with a Kleenex.

The other woman raised a perfectly shaped blond brow. "Is it? Then how do you explain that his eyes are always on you?"

"Are you feeling all right?" Sara queried.

"Of course."

"No headaches, dizzy spells, nothing like that?"

"No. Why do you ask?"

"Because that's a very fanciful notion for an Ice Queen."

"That's merely my name when I am on the trapeze," Helga countered. "And just because I'm not as publicly demonstrative as some people, you should not get the mistaken idea that I do not understand passion. Or that I cannot recognize it when I see it in your writer."

"He is *not* my writer," Sara repeated firmly. Finding herself unable to sit still, she began pacing the canvas floor of the tent. "And as for this alleged passion, how do you explain the fact that the man hasn't even attempted to be alone with me for eight days?" Her tone was sharp with feminine pique.

Helga left the incriminating sentence hanging in the air for a long, significant moment. "He wants to make love to you, *ja?*"

"Yes." Sara dragged her hands through her hair as she marched back and forth. "No."

More than a little amused, Helga watched as Sara sank into the overstuffed wing chair, the only concession to comfort in the tent. Sara had insisted on dragging the chair from town to town for the past five summers. It had been patched innumerable times, yet fluffy gray stuffing continued to seep out onto the canvas floor around it.

"*Ja. Nein.* Which is it?"

Irritation, frustration and something Sara unwillingly recognized as desire prickled beneath her skin.

She practically leaped from the chair to resume her pacing. "Neither. Both. Damn."

Sara had never thought of herself as a nervous person. Energetic, perhaps. Animated. But never nervous. Until now. Until Darius Wilde had come into her life and tied her stomach into knots.

"He has you confused," Helga decided, placing her cup on an overturned plastic milk crate serving as a table.

The compact interior of the tent was not meant for walking off tension. Sara reached the far end in a few long strides and spun around, her eyes revealing her inner turmoil. "He told me that he was going to make love to me almost immediately after we'd met."

"You make it sound as if he gave you little choice in the matter."

"*He* behaved as if I had none at all," she countered briskly, her cheeks flaming as she recalled his easy masculine self-confidence. What if she had given in that night at his loft? Sara wondered, certainly not for the first time since leaving Philadelphia. Once he had satisfied his curiosity, would Darius have left her and gone on to newer, more exciting conquests? Or would she have spent these past seven nights in his arms, instead of tossing and turning on a too-hard, too-narrow army surplus cot?

"His behavior infuriated you?"

"Wouldn't it you?" Sara refilled her cup, knowing that the additional caffeine was probably going to keep her awake. Not that it really mattered; if tonight turned out to be like all the others, forbidden, erotic thoughts of Darius Wilde would prevent her from sleeping, anyway.

Helga put her hand over her own mug, signaling that she'd had enough. "Of course it would," she agreed easily. "Even if a woman wishes to make love to a man, she wants to feel that she has a choice, *ja*?"

Sara nodded. "Exactly."

In the muted glow of the kerosene lantern Helga was able to see the shadows under Sara's eyes. They'd been getting darker day by day, and unless she was mistaken, her friend had lost at least five pounds. Not that it was any wonder—from what Helga could tell, Sara had been living solely on tea, coffee and diet cola ever since the tour had begun.

Recalling her own stormy courtship with her hot-tempered, single-minded Russian husband, Helga's amusement turned to compassion.

"So, although a very strong part of you played the role of reluctant maiden, you secretly expected Darius to lay siege. To increase his seduction attempts. To, how do you say it, pull out all the stoppers?"

"Stops," Sara corrected wearily. "And yes, I suppose that's what I expected."

Helga rose from the folding chair in a lithe, smooth movement that was the result of a youth spent in ballet classes and an inherent grace she'd had since her birth thirty-one years before.

"We did not meet until after I had married my Yuri," she said quietly, putting her hand on Sara's arm. "So you did not witness my husband's exhausting manner of courting a woman."

Sara managed a weak smile. "I've no doubt Yuri would have displayed his own enthusiasm, sweeping you off your feet and into bed at the same time."

Helga laughed. "He tried, with his unique flair. But I was the famed Ice Queen, star of the Circus Knie. I had my reputation to protect."

"So you resisted," Sara guessed.

Helga's smile was softly reminiscent. "*Ja*. I resisted. We continued that way whenever our paths crossed. Yuri would stage his own version of the blitzkrieg; I would resist. Attack and retreat. It went on that way for months."

"At least he didn't give up," Sara grumbled.

"Oh, but he did. One day, in Lucerne, shortly after he had defected, he lost his temper in the lobby of the Tivoli Hotel." She shook her head, her lips curved in amusement. "Oh, Sara, it was indeed a sight to behold; he shouted, he screamed, he threw things. Before the man was finished, he had managed to get us both thrown out of the hotel."

"And then?" Caught up in the story, Sara momentarily forgot her own problems.

Helga shrugged. "And then he left."

"But he came back."

"He says now that he would have," Helga agreed. "After a sufficient period of time spent sulking like some deposed Russian czar. But at the time I had no way of knowing that. After six long and sleepless weeks of suffering, I discovered where he was and confronted him at a lodge in the Bavarian Alps where I found him nursing a skiing injury. He'd broken his leg in three places."

"Poor Yuri."

The other woman made a sound of sheer disgust. "Do not waste your time feeling sorry for the man; you were not there to see all the willing women eager to assist in his recovery."

Sara bit back a grin when the usually composed woman displayed a flare of temper at the memory. "What did you do?"

"Why, what any normal woman would do, when upon discovering her beloved lounging like a pasha in the midst of his harem, of course. I screamed at him."

"You didn't!"

"Of course I did. And I threatened to pull out the hair of all the women by its roots."

"I can't believe that," Sara protested.

"It was necessary to threaten them in order to make them leave," Helga explained simply. "Once they had evacuated the premises, I spent the next ten minutes throwing pewter beer steins at the bastard." An unholy gleam appeared in her ice-blue eyes. "Actually, he moved quite fast, for a man whose left leg was encased in plaster all the way to his hip."

"I find it difficult to believe that you, of all people would create a scene."

"We were thrown out of the lodge," Helga said proudly. "Three days later we were married."

"And in the interim?"

Helga flashed her a warm, knowing smile. "What do you think?"

Sara downed her tea, then refilled her cup once again. "I envy you," she murmured. "And I think that you are both very lucky."

"And so will you be," Helga replied with the air of composed self-confidence she wore like a second skin. "You and your writer."

She patted Sara's cheek, then turned, gliding from the tent before Sara could complain yet again that Darius Wilde was *not* her writer.

6

FOR TWO WEEKS the rigorous schedule remained the same: the circus would arrive in a town on Friday afternoon, and everyone would help set up the equipment. The troupe would perform two shows on Saturday, two more on Sunday. Sunday night they'd strike, drive to the next town on Monday, set up Monday night for shows on Tuesday and Wednesday, strike Thursday, then move on to the next setup on Friday, where the procedure would begin all over again.

If Sara saw less of Darius than she would have liked, she was always aware of his presence as he worked in the cook-tent, drove the equipment truck and even proved adept at rewiring the overhead lights when a generator failed in New Galilee.

He fit in well, she admitted. No job was too dirty or too hard, and if at times she found herself wishing that he'd resume his earlier seduction campaign, she assured herself that, in the long run, it was probably all for the best.

It was a little after six o'clock in the morning on the fifteenth day when they entered Iowa. The Hawkeye State was decidedly hilly—the landscape curved sensually, horizons undulated, hills rolled in and out of each other like gentle ocean swells. Tractors made their way across the green fields, creating stunning geometric patterns on acre after acre of the rich, fertile land. Horses grazed contentedly.

Two hours later the caravan reached Pella, their stopover for the next three days. Despite her brave words about avoiding involvement, Sara couldn't resist watching Darius drive the huge tent stakes into the ground with a sledgehammer. His body glowed with a healthy sheen of perspiration as he lifted the hammer and swung it downward, unerringly hitting the broad metal head of the stake.

When her fingers practically itched to reach out and stroke that strong, dark back, she curled them into fists at her sides. It was better this way, she reminded herself firmly. Safer. Then he looked up at her, and Sara knew that there was no refuge from her feelings for this man.

Darius couldn't begin to count the number of times he'd thought of Sara during the past two long and frustrating weeks. With a willpower he didn't know he had, he'd forced himself to keep busy, volunteering for any job, no matter how physically demanding, in the hope that it might drive the erotic fantasies from his mind. But even when his muscles ached with unaccustomed strain at the end of the day, his mind continued to dwell on the softness of her skin, the seductive allure of her scent.

If he had been troubled with thoughts of Sara during the day, the nights had been nothing less than agony. It had taken every ounce of his self-control to keep from marching across the compound to her tent, flinging her down onto the floor and making love to her all night long, until both of them were too exhausted, and much too satisfied, to move.

What kept Darius from acting out that enticing fantasy was that he had determined early on that Sara McBride was a woman accustomed to making her own decisions. That she had been doing so for some time was obvious. That she would continue to do so was also evident. Watching her cajole, flatter and, when necessary, argue in order to get her way over the past two weeks, he had come to doubt that she had ever learned the meaning of the word no, except to see it as yet another challenge to overcome.

That knowledge informed him that she must have driven her family crazy from time to time. If told something was hot, the child Sara would have needed to touch, in order to see for herself. But what her conservative parents had obviously considered a distressing bent toward noncomformity, Darius found entrancing.

The trick to handling Sara Cornell McBride, he had determined, was not handling her at all. If he left her alone, continued to maintain his distance, she would eventually have to come to him. And once she did, he was not going to let her get away.

As their unwavering gazes locked and held, Sara's mouth went dry. For what seemed an eternity but was no more than ten seconds, neither blinked as an unspoken challenge electrified the air around them. When he finally smiled, a slow, dangerous smile that spoke volumes, Sara's skin prickled with goose bumps, then went warm all over.

Rewarded by the recognition that flashed in her eyes, Darius crossed the space between them, his gaze not moving from her face. Even in the bright, fault-revealing light of morning he found her exceptionally lovely.

"Good morning."

His voice flowed over her, warm and inviting. Sara felt the deep tug of a need that had been too long denied. "Good morning," she responded, a bit more breathlessly than she would have liked.

"Nice day."

"Isn't it?"

She had been going crazy for two weeks, and now that they finally had a minute alone, he wanted to talk about the weather? Didn't he know what he was doing to her? Didn't he realize that she was drawn to him, as she had never been drawn to any man before?

"The radio announcers are predicting rain for tomorrow." Her creamy skin had tanned golden from her long days in the sun, and the soft hue of late summer roses bloomed in her cheeks. Darius was tempted to crush his mouth against those gently smiling lips and taste the mellow morning sunshine in them.

Sara shrugged. "We've performed in the rain before. We're a sturdy lot here at the Peter and Wendy Family Circus and Penguin Extravaganza; none of us melted."

He moved closer, until they were standing toe to toe. "Yuri says you've played here before."

Underneath the faint scent of perspiration, Sara detected the sharp aroma of soap. As she stared up into his eyes, she realized on some distant level that their breathing had become synchronized.

"It's our third summer at the Tulip Festival," she said. "Last year Yuri added an act that le petit Diable, Paulo Redige, made famous. He danced on the rope in a pair of wooden shoes, then when the music ended, leaped up in the air, broke the shoes by clapping his heels together and landed back on the rope in his stocking feet. The audience here is predominantly Dutch; needless to say, they loved it."

"I can imagine." Had it not been for the sparks in the air surrounding them, they could have been strangers, chatting casually while waiting for a bus. Darius restrained himself from grinding his teeth even as he admitted to himself that if he didn't have her soon, he'd go insane.

"I think he's planning to do the trick again this year," she informed him.

"I'm looking forward to seeing it."

A soft breeze blew a coppery cloud of hair across her eyes. Darius reached up and brushed it away. The touch, as casual as it was, shot through her. Sara decided it was time to retreat before she allowed him to see how strongly his touch, his very presence, affected her. Unused to restraining her emotions, she was finding the continuous effort exhausting.

"Well, if you'll excuse me, Darius, I have a great deal of work to do. After all, we're on a tight schedule and—"

His fingers curved around her wrist as she prepared to turn away. "Sara." It was only her name, but it had the power to stop her in her tracks.

She swallowed. "Yes?"

"I happen to know that we're ahead of schedule. In fact, according to Helga and Yuri, you don't have a single thing to do until tomorrow afternoon's performance."

As his thumb rubbed against the silky skin on the inside of her wrist, Sara's pulse speeded up. She wondered if he'd noticed; one wary glance upward at his gleaming dark eyes confirmed that he had.

"Helga and Yuri don't know all my plans," she insisted. "Besides, they have their own reasons . . ." Her voice trailed off as she realized that she was on the brink of revealing too much.

Darius lifted her hand to his lips. "You were about to mention their belief that we would be good together."

"No," she lied. "I wasn't. I mean, they don't believe anything of the sort."

He smiled. "No wonder you always lose whenever you play poker with the tumbling Manconi brothers; you're not a very agile liar, Sara. Your eyes give you away. Every time. You couldn't bluff even if you wanted to."

Her pulse was pounding. Sara's brain gave the message to her body to pull away. Now. Before he was able to read all her secrets. But her mutinous body steadfastly ignored the desperate command.

Confusion, mingling with desire, swirled in the depths of her eyes. "What do you want from me?"

"I thought you'd never ask." His grin was quick and nonthreatening, at odds with the meltingly seductive touch of his lips as they grazed her knuckles enticingly. "I'd like to steal a few hours to visit the Tulip Festival."

"With me?"

"Who else around here could possibly compete with acres and acres of dazzling, fragrant flowers? How about it, Sara? I've taken part in cultural ceremonies in some of the most remote locations of the world, but I have never had the good fortune to attend a Tulip Festival; I don't want to experience it for the first time alone."

Her nerves on edge from the constant struggle to camouflage her unruly emotions, Sara allowed her pleasure to show. "I'd love to share it with you."

Flashing her a pleased grin, Darius released her hand. "Terrific. Give me ten minutes to clean up and I'll meet you at your tent."

After suffering through fourteen nights of unfulfilled erotic fantasies in the close confines of that very tent, Sara didn't trust herself to be alone with him there. "Why don't I meet you back here instead," she suggested.

She really should be more circumspect, Darius considered as he watched desire war with reluctant propriety on her upturned face. But if she were, if she learned to conceal her vibrant feelings, she wouldn't be his Sara. And after a lifetime spent carefully avoiding commitments of all kinds, he wouldn't have fallen head over heels with a free-spirited gypsy who had made him forget any other woman he'd ever known.

"Whatever you say," he agreed easily.

THE BRISK CLICK CLACK of wooden shoes on pavement. The wet scratching of stiff-bristled brooms as traditionally costumed street scrubbers prepared the parade route for the Tulip Queen. Windmills surrounded by fields of dazzling color. Familiar cup-shaped flowers in beds stretching as far as the eye could see—scarlet, indigo, saffron, snow-white—looking like the gaily colored ribbons of a Maypole rippling in the gentle breeze.

Sara had reveled in the joyous community celebration before, but never had it meant as much to her as it did today. She wasn't foolish enough to try to tell herself that her enjoyment was due to anything other than that she was sharing the bright spring day with Darius.

"Oh, look," she said, drawn to a vendor selling a variety of chocolates, "chocolate-covered strawberries! My very favorite thing in the entire world."

"I thought the chocolate-covered cherries you bought down the street were your very favorite thing in the entire world," he pointed out. "And before that it was chocolate pretzels. And before that—"

"It was chocolate fudge," she interrupted with a grin. "I know, I'm incorrigible, but the aroma drives me absolutely mad. I simply can't resist." She dimpled at the vendor, a dour man Darius guessed to be in his late sixties. "However do you stand it? I'd have eaten all my stock before the sun came up this morning. And they'd have to carry me home in a wheelbarrow."

"I manage to resist temptation," the man answered in a deadpan voice that made Darius suspect he had just run across the only man in the world capable of withstanding Sara's dazzling smile. "That will be two dollars."

Sara shook her head as she handed over her money and accepted the small white bag. "You certainly have a great deal more willpower than I do," she said admiringly. "Have you entered these in the judging?" she asked as she took a sample bite.

"*Ja,*"."

Sara rolled her eyes appreciatively as she allowed the blend of smooth chocolate and sweet berry to linger on her tongue. "I'm so glad; they're absolutely heavenly. If you don't win first prize, the contest is definitely rigged and you should insist on a recount. Well, goodbye," she said gaily, her attention momentarily captured by a small girl selling tulips wrapped in green tissue paper.

"Miss!"

Sara turned back. "Yes?"

The man reached under the counter and pulled out a tray of the largest strawberries Darius had ever seen. "For you," he insisted. "*Dehagen.* Take one."

The smile that Darius knew would still have the power to thrill him when he was seventy bloomed on her face. "Why, thank you," she said, selecting a berry the size of a child's fist. "My goodness, wasn't that sweet of him?" she asked Darius as they walked away.

"Sweet," he agreed dryly, stopping to purchase a bouquet of red and yellow tulips.

"Oh, aren't they lovely," she exclaimed. "Thank you, Darius."

"My pleasure. And by the way, congratulations."

"Congratulations?"

"When we walked up to that guy, he reminded me of the doorman at the House of Usher. By the time you bought your strawberries, you had him looking as if he'd been run over by a Mack truck. And had enjoyed every second of it."

"Oh, pooh," she complained. "You're just jealous because he didn't give you a free sample. Here." She held it up to him, her blue eyes a sparkling invitation. "Take a bite. You'll be crazy about it. I promise."

"You just want to go back to the circus and boast to everyone that you had me eating out of your hand."

She grinned. "Absolutely."

Unable to deny her anything, Darius took a sample bite. It was sweet and juicy and everything she'd promised. And it only left him wanting more.

"Not bad."

"Not bad?" Sara looked at him argumentatively. "That just goes to show what an indiscriminating palate you have, Darius Wilde. Perhaps you just need another taste."

His eyes darkened to jet as they settled on her berry-stained mouth. "Perhaps I do."

In one smooth move he gathered her close and captured her smiling lips. The kiss ended as quickly as it had begun, but neither Darius nor Sara managed to remain unaffected. The long look they exchanged hinted at things yet to come—secrets to be discovered, pledges to be exchanged.

"You're right," he drawled, skimming his knuckles gently down the side of her face. "The taste is incomparable."

Sara stared up at him as her head continued to spin. She'd never known they had earthquakes in Iowa. If it hadn't been an earthquake, she considered with a long, slow blink, then she was definitely sunk. "I take it back."

Although he had been as stunned as Sara by the power of what should have been a light, playful kiss, Darius hid it better. "Take what back?" he questioned, a smile teasing at the corners of his lips. "The kiss? I'd say it's a little late for that, sweetheart."

"Not the kiss. I liked that. I meant that I take back what I said about your apparent inability to appreciate certain flavors." Her eyes twinkled as humor returned to shut off other emotions better left untapped. For now. "You appear to be a man of gourmet tastes, after all, Darius."

He put a friendly arm around her shoulders as they continued down the street. "You know, now that you mention it, lately I seemed to have developed an insatiable sweet tooth," he agreed cheerfully.

It was lunchtime when **they re**turned to the campground. Reluctant to have the pleasant day end so soon, Sara immediately accepted Darius's suggestion that they drive out to nearby Red Rock Lake for a picnic. After a visit to the cook-tent for supplies and a stop at a gas station to fill up the van that had been assigned to

Darius for the past week, after another performer had taken his turn at driving the big truck, they were off.

As they drove along the road through the fields, the new green grass swayed in the soft breeze. There were tall white houses with wide front porches where you could imagine the rusty squeak of screen doors on the mellow spring breeze. In one yard she watched a small black-and-white dog tugging energetically at sheets on a clothesline. From his smile, Sara knew that Darius shared her enjoyment of the simple scene.

"Looks like we're going to get that rain a little earlier than expected," Darius remarked, casting a glance up at the pewter sky.

"It would be better if the storm passed before tomorrow afternoon's performance."

"It won't do much for our picnic."

Sara shrugged unconcernedly. "The company's the important thing. Not the weather."

He reached out and covered her hand with his. "I like a lady who knows her priorities."

Sara returned his smile. For now no further words were necessary.

Although the rain held off long enough to allow them to enjoy a lunch of chicken sandwiches, thick slices of icy watermelon and glasses of chilled California Chablis provided by the obliging Yuri, the threat of inclement weather seemed to be keeping others from the lake. A single sailboat sped across the whitecapped waves, its red sail fluttering gaily in the breeze.

"There's something I've been meaning to ask you," Sara said late that afternoon. "Something I don't understand."

Darius was leaning back on his elbows on the blue-and-black plaid blanket, watching Sara with unabashed pleasure as she managed to make an entire plate of rich chocolate brownies disappear like magic.

"That makes two of us."

She licked some gooey fudge frosting off her fingers. "Excuse me?"

"With all the sweets you eat, I can't figure out why you aren't the fat lady in the Peter and Wendy Circus."

"Careful, Darius," Sara warned lightly. "With lines like that you're just liable to sweep a girl right off her feet." Leaning forward, she pressed a quick kiss onto his smiling lips. There was an instantaneous flash of heat. And then she backed away.

"My turn." Darius tangled his fingers in the riotous red-gold waves of her hair and drew her unprotestingly down to him.

He nibbled idly at her lips, tasting his way from one corner of her mouth to the other, steadfastly resisting Sara's attempts to deepen the kiss. "You taste like temptation," he murmured as the tip of his tongue dampened her bottom lip. "Sweet. And warm." His tongue skimmed up her jaw to circle her ear, causing Sara's thoughts to tangle. "Ripe."

"Darius . . ."

"I like to hear you say my name," he murmured, punctuating his soft words with slow, melting kisses. "Say it again."

His hands had slipped under the hem of her blue-and-white striped cotton sweater and his lean, strong fingers were tracing ever-widening circles on the soft flesh just below her rib cage. Sara trembled. "Darius."

His kisses remained featherlight, his hands gentle as they drew her deeper and deeper into a gold realm of sensation. "Again," he said as he lowered her to the plush blanket.

His clever fingers slid up her rib cage, then increasingly higher, his slow, seductive touch seeming to melt the wispy scrap of indigo covering her breasts. When those fingers plucked at her taut, lace-covered nipples, Sara felt a deep, answering pull between her thighs and sighed his name through slightly parted lips.

When he lowered his head, teasing the tingling bud with his lips, his tongue, Sara's heart hammered beneath his mouth and she arched toward him, seeking to soothe the aching fullness in her breast. Although his own body was throbbing with a desperate need of its own, Darius continued to take his time, drawing her slowly, unerringly, into the mists.

He wanted her; he'd wanted her for weeks. But it had been important that their lovemaking spring from her own needs and not his. Now, listening to her faint, inarticulate sounds of pleasure, Darius knew that the waiting had been worthwhile.

Sara was floating on gentle waves of ecstasy, marveling at sensations she had never known. Her body felt fluid, pliant under his touch, languid and warm. So very, very warm. His hands, his mouth, the foolish, seductive words he murmured in her ear, made her feet as if she were melting.

The dark clouds overhead rumbled; Sara thought it was the sound of her heated blood pounding in her head. The brilliant flash of lightning in the slate-gray sky seemed nothing more than the exploding sensations behind her half-closed lids. The light moisture on her skin went ignored as his lips caressed her face.

"You're getting wet," he murmured, pressing his mouth against her damp hair.

"Mmm. Kiss me again."

He brushed his lips against hers.

"No, not that way." Her arms felt like leaden weights as she put them around his neck. "Really kiss me."

Darius obliged her willingly, feeling his hunger build for a long, rapturous time as he tasted the passion laced with rain on her small, avid mouth. "You are exquisite," he said, brushing his lips up her cheekbones. "Absolutely exquisite."

"I'm so glad you approve."

"Hmm, I do."

Her lips curved in a slow, bemused smile. "Good. Are we finally going to make love now?"

Looking down into her softly flushed face, viewing the unmistakable desire in her heart-melting gaze, Darius felt as if he were slowly, inexorably sinking into quicksand. "Aren't you worried about catching pneumonia out here?"

"Not at all." Her fingers skimmed along his firm jaw. "You'll keep me warm."

"Granted, I'll do my best," he agreed pleasantly. "But I feel obliged to point out that so far I haven't had much success keeping you dry." He ran his hand down her wet and tangled hair.

"I hadn't noticed."

Darius grinned as the cool rain and a surge of good humor conspired to bank his desire temporarily. "I think I'll take that as a compliment."

"Good, because that's how I meant it." She glanced over at the van parked nearby. "You do have a point about the pneumonia, I suppose."

"Wouldn't want to take any unnecessary chances," he agreed.

"After all, it is rather chilly."

"Downright cold for the end of May."

"And we are rather wet."

Darius ran his hand down the front of her sodden sweater. "Drenched."

Sara's eyes, as they smiled up at him, made it seem as if the sun had suddenly escaped from behind the dark clouds. "I suppose," she said slowly, "that the very least we should do, in the name of preventive medicine, would be to get out of these wet clothes."

Darius grinned as he rose to his feet, pulling Sara with him. "Sweetheart, I thought you'd never ask."

Hand in hand, they ran, laughing, toward the van.

7

"I NEVER DID get a chance to ask you my question," Sara said once they'd changed into dry clothing—he into a pair of faded jeans and a gray sweatshirt that had seen better days while she settled for an Irish fisherman's sweater that fell halfway down her thighs.

Although only minutes ago they had been on the verge of making love, the seductive mood seemed to have dissipated for the moment. Neither Sara nor Darius regretted its passing; they knew that their lovemaking was inevitable, that there was no reason to hurry. For now they were content to sip coffee and gaze out at the slanting rain.

"That's right," he recalled. "There was something about me you didn't understand."

More than one thing, Sara corrected silently. For starters, what was it about him that tempted her to risk her heart even when she knew it could only be broken in the end?

"All your other books—even the ones written for a mass market, like *Drumbeats*—have reflected your anthropological training. So why would you want to profile a circus—especially one like ours?"

"What do you mean, especially one like yours?"

"Well, we're certainly not Ringling Brothers."

Darius frowned. "Damn. I hadn't noticed. Are you telling me that you don't have three rings?"

"Only one."

"And you don't have any lions, tigers or bears?"

"Nary a lion nor a tiger," Sara said with feigned regret. "And our bears are cancan dancers in fuzzy brown suits and tutus."

"Damn. You're right. I don't know why I'm wasting my time with you when I could be traveling the country in style."

"Perhaps you like the way I kiss?"

Darius slapped his palm against his forehead. "By Jove, I think she's got it." He bent his head and brushed his lips against her smiling ones.

"Really," Sara insisted softly. "I want to understand. I think I *need* to understand."

"It's not all that complicated," he said. "In the first place, this book isn't that different from many of my others. They've all dealt with history and roots, which the circus definitely has. For instance, in 421 B.C. there was a dinner party given in Athens by a wealthy dilettante by the name of Callias. Everyone who was anyone was there, including Socrates. Sometime during the evening the dinner was interrupted by a troupe of entertainers—jesters, mimes, jugglers." He smiled. "Probably a great deal like the members of the Peter and Wendy Family Circus and Penguin Extravaganza."

"Ah, but I'll bet they didn't have dancers dressed up like penguins," Sara pointed out.

"Probably not," he agreed easily. "Or at least if they did, certainly not ones who danced as if they'd just tapped their way out of a Busby Berkeley musical. Anyway, five hundred years later, during a banquet in Rome, a troupe of rope dancers and acrobats entertained. One rope walker leaped through an iron hoop around which blazing torches had been fixed."

"Like Yuri."

Darius nodded. "Exactly. So, you see, the circus has history. It has roots. The multitalented people I've met during the past two weeks could easily have been medieval minstrels, playing the roles of musicians, jesters, acrobats, jugglers, conjurers—"

"We have to play a lot of parts," she pointed out. "Because we don't have the funds to increase the number of performers on payroll."

"But that's what I mean," Darius insisted, warming to the idea. "Your circus, Sara, reminds me of the little bands of entertainers wandering through Europe in the Middle Ages, playing in castles every so often, but more likely gathering at village greens to perform for the townspeople."

"I think I would have liked performing at a castle," Sara mused.

"You would have stolen the show. Although it would have been the end of your career."

She arched a challenging copper brow. "Really? Why?" If he was daring to suggest that she wasn't talented enough to perform for royalty, Sara was going to dump her cooling coffee over his head.

Darius saw the temper in her expression and had to bite back a grin. "Because the moment you sashayed into the room, sweetheart, the king would have insisted on having you. Then after you were married, you would have been too busy with queenly duties—such as providing his lordship with heirs and seeing to the royal rose gardens—to continue your travels, so your circus would have fallen apart for lack of inspiration and there you'd be, trapped forever in a golden throne room."

"That's a nice thing to say," Sara said with a pleased smile. "Except being trapped in the throne room, of course."

"Of course."

"But I suppose that comes with being married."

"You view marriage and children as a trap?" Darius asked, knowing that they were getting off the track but suddenly very interested in Sara's response.

Sara heard the sudden sharpness in Darius's tone and wondered at its cause. "For some."

"You can't tell me that you believe Helga and Yuri consider themselves trapped."

"Well, no—"

"Or Germaine and Philip?"

"They were ecstatic. In fact, there was a time, shortly after Philip died of that heart attack three years ago, that I was honestly afraid Germaine would crumble into pieces."

"Of course she didn't."

"She's a remarkably stalwart woman," Sara agreed. "But she did adore Philip."

"Enough to give up her career to move to the States with him. And I certainly don't remember ever receiving the impression that she felt the slightest bit trapped by her decision."

"Not all women are as self-confident as Germaine," Sara felt obliged to point out. "Some might need their own career. Their own life."

"Is that what went wrong with your own marriage?" Darius asked recklessly.

Sara felt an all-too-familiar knife twisting in her heart. She slowly lowered the cup to the table with trembling hands. "I really don't want to talk about my marriage," she protested quietly.

Darius felt like swearing as he watched Sara's emotional shield go up. "Well, is that what happened? Did you feel trapped? Did you need your own life?"

"Please," she said in a whisper.

She was wringing her hands, but immersed in his own building frustration, Darius failed to notice. "Did you experience a desperate need to escape your husband's house, Sara? His bed? Were you afraid that having his children would keep you from traveling with your precious circus?"

As soon as he'd said the scathing words, Darius regretted them. How had a casual discussion about circus history dissolved into a personal attack on the one woman he'd cut off his right arm to avoid hurting?

She'd gone as white as a sheet. "You don't understand; honestly, you have it all wrong."

He put an arm around her, drawing her to him. She was cold. Too cold. "Sara, I'm sorry. I don't know what got into me."

Wondering what had made her ever think that she could escape the ghosts of her past, Sara tried to control the tremor in her voice. "I didn't leave Jeremy; he left me."

It crossed Darius's mind that although Jeremy McBride was obviously an ass, if his own behavior a moment ago were any example, he couldn't be considered a hell of a lot better.

A single tear slid down her cheek. Darius brushed it away with his finger. "Honey, I was out of line."

She was staring unseeingly at the silver curtain of rain. "No," she corrected in a ragged whisper. "I was. That's what he always said."

Her obviously stricken state was coming as a shock. Darius was accustomed to Sara's sunshine. Her warmth. If he ever met the man who still possessed the power to turn her life dark and cold, Darius vowed he'd put his fist right through the bastard's face.

"It's over, Sara," he insisted, pressing his lips into her still-damp hair. "In the past. It's history; it doesn't matter any longer."

The eyes she lifted up to him were as dark and bleak as a tomb. "You don't understand," she protested, shaking her head as she wrenched out of his arms and struggled to her feet. "No one does."

Secrets. He never would have imagined her possessing them. She seemed so open. So totally without guile. Yet whatever she was determined to keep from him was obviously tearing her apart. Darius caught her arm as she swayed dangerously.

"Come lie down," he insisted with studied calm. "Before you fall down."

Her lips were so very, very dry. And her head ached with a dull, throbbing pain. And her heart. Sara pressed her palm against her chest. Dear God, her heart seemed to be breaking in two.

"I'm fine," she insisted, but nevertheless she allowed him to lead her to the fold-out bunk at the rear of the van.

"Of course you are," he agreed easily. "In fact, you're a helluva lot better than fine. You're exquisite, remember? But that won't keep you from landing flat on your face when you faint, sweetheart."

As she stretched out on the bed, Darius's eyes settled on her long, smooth legs. A hot, unbidden flash of need shot through him even as he asked himself what kind of man he could be to be experiencing sexual desire when it was obvious that Sara was distraught.

The mattress sighed as he sat down on the edge. "Want to talk about it?" he asked, lifting strands of hair away from her ashen face.

Unable to bear the compassion on his face, Sara turned her head away. "I can't," she murmured into the pillow.

Darius reminded himself, with effort, that he had already decided not to push Sara into anything she wasn't ready for. "All right," he agreed calmly. "We'll just sit here and listen to the rain on the roof."

"We should be getting back. Everyone will wonder where we are."

"I think they'll have a pretty good idea. After all, I haven't exactly been hiding how I felt about you these past two weeks."

"You haven't once tried to be alone with me," she complained softly.

"I didn't dare. Not without taking the chance of embarrassing a lot of innocent bystanders; in case you haven't noticed, sweetheart, there's not a lot of privacy around the Peter and Wendy Family Circus and Penguin Extravaganza. Every time a member of the troupe so much as sneezes, twenty-five voices call out gesundheit. Shoot, whenever Mario drinks a second beer at dinner, his snoring keeps half the crew awake."

The idea that he'd been thinking of her these long, lonely days and nights helped ease the shattering pain she'd been experiencing. Sara worried that if she opened herself up to all Darius seemed to be offering, the inevitable pain, when it finally came, would be almost unbearable. But not impossible to bear. She would survive it. As she had survived others, even more devastating than a broken romance.

"I'm glad you weren't ignoring me, Darius."

There it was again—that sweet openness that made it so difficult to believe that Sara would be capable of emotional subterfuge. Darius stifled a long, weary sigh as he accepted the fact that even with Sara McBride, things were often not quite what they seemed.

He stretched out beside her and took her in his arms. They remained that way for a long, silent time, the only sounds were the pitter-patter of the rain on the van roof and their own slow, steady breathing. Sara was beginning to suspect that Darius had fallen asleep when he began to speak.

"I grew up in northern Arizona. My mother's maiden name was Mary Cody; she's a White Mountain Apache and a teacher on the reservation there. My father's a doctor; they met when he moved west to establish a medical clinic. She's a quiet, gentle woman; he has a long fuse, but when it finally blows, his temper can knock you right off the face of the earth. As different as their personalities are, they've been happily married for forty years."

"That's nice," she murmured.

"I've always thought so. When I was about six years old, my parents took me to my first circus. Thinking back on it, I realize that it wasn't a very good one. There was one tent, five performers, a swaybacked dapple-gray horse and a scruffy yellow dog of undistinguishable parentage. But they drove into town in this bright yellow truck, with a guy standing on a platform in the back blowing a trumpet for all he was worth while his teenage daughters, dressed in bright red satin, twirled flaming batons as they marched down the street.

"It was as if they transformed everything with their energy and flashiness: the town, the people, even, in many ways, my life. Payson, a small town in the Arizona mountains, had suddenly become a celebration; they were sorcerers, magicians. One minute they were there, and then they were gone. They were like the crazy uncle, the one the family never approves of, who comes to visit every December, with his jokes and songs and slapstick routines."

"The one you always miss when he's gone," Sara murmured.

He brushed his lips against her temple. "That's it. Exactly. And when they disappeared, it was as if they'd left a trail of magic stardust behind them. Like so many other kids, I began to dream of running away to join the circus."

"And now you finally have."

"And now I finally have," he agreed. Their eyes met and there was a moment of heat. "You know that I want you."

"Yes," she whispered.

Her enticing scent floated on the rain-softened air, filling his head like a fragrant cloud, fogging his senses, making coherent thought difficult. Darius reminded himself that this time—the first time—he'd promised himself that he would do things right. That he would not permit his needs—or hers—to rush him.

He traced the line of her cheek with a finger, stunned to find that his hands were far from steady. "So much . . ." His other hand was slowly lifting the hem of the heavy sweater, inching it up her legs. "I ache for you, Sara."

She turned her head, pressing her lips against his hand. "I've wanted you, too, Darius. From the beginning, I think."

Inch by inch the sweater rose, revealing the luxurious satin of her skin. When he pulled it over her head, Sara shifted to help him, murmuring soft, inarticulate words of encouragement.

As much as he wanted her, there was one more vital thing Darius had to consider. "Sara," he murmured urgently against her lips. "Is this all right?"

Sara couldn't think of anything in the world that would be more right than the feelings she was experiencing at this moment. "Oh, yes," she said with a breathless sigh.

He lifted his head, looking down at her with a tenderness that she knew she'd never be able to forget, whatever happened between them. "I mean is it safe? Are you protected, sweetheart?"

She blinked at she sought to decipher his words. Safe? Her body was, perhaps; knowing that their lovemaking was inevitable, she'd seen to the matter of birth control before leaving Philadelphia. But her heart . . . Now that was an entirely different matter.

"Yes." She ran her fingers through his hair, urging his lips back to hers. "Yes, yes, yes."

Her eyelids fluttered closed, but through her swirling senses she could feel him caressing her yearning body with soft, openmouthed kisses that caused her blood to run more quickly in her veins.

His lips and hands were never still, moving over her warming flesh, leaving sparks in their wake. Wherever his lips touched, she burned; wherever his hands stroked, she flamed. Her body was pliant, yielding wherever he touched her. Coherent thought disintegrated, consumed by the firestorm that had taken over her mind.

Growing desperate, she moved under him, her hands delving under the gray sweatshirt to roam across his back. Smooth muscles rippled sensuously under her racing fingertips, and when she slipped her questing hands between the faded denim and his hot, moist skin, Darius's hips surged forward, driving her deeper still into the thin mattress of the bunk.

They were caught in a wildfire of their own making as Darius's desire soared with hers. With one hand never ceasing its heated caresses, he managed to dispatch his clothing with the other. Free of the barrier of material between them, Sara gasped as she felt her hot flesh against his. No longer languid, no longer content to remain passive, her hands and mouth rushed over him. The inner flames continued to build as her fingers explored the hard ridges and lean planes of his body without inhibition and her lips drank in the passion-moist taste of his skin.

Heat flowed out of her, surrounding his senses until Darius no longer remembered his vow to linger, to savor. His mouth scorched a trail of moist fire down her body, his tongue tormenting her with a need that made her lift her hips off the mattress as she desperately sought relief.

Gasping out her name, Darius took possession of Sara, his strong, greedy thrusts driving her deeper and deeper into a smoke-filled netherworld, which finally exploded with a blinding glare of dazzling light and glowing heat.

LYING IN THE WARM afterglow of passion, neither Darius nor Sara appeared willing to be the first one to break the hush that had settled over their world. His hand rested lightly on her breast; Sara's short, unpainted fingernails traced idle patterns on the dark skin of his thigh. Just as she had never known such passion, Sara couldn't ever remember feeling such contentment. When he nibbled lightly at her neck, she sighed; when his lips trailed along the soft slope of her shoulder, she trembled.

"Cold?"

Sara shook her head. "Not at all." Her softly flushed face glowed with the memory of their recent lovemaking. "I never knew it could be like that."

Darius propped himself up on one elbow as he brushed her love-tousled hair away from her face. "Neither did I."

Her answering smile was positively beatific. "How do you always know exactly the right thing to say?"

He bent his head and kissed her cheek. "Perhaps because in this case it's the truth. It was special because *you're* special, Sara."

Sara wanted nothing more than to believe him. She wanted to believe that what had happened between them was as unique as it was wonderful. She wanted to believe it with every fiber of her being. So for now, for this bliss-filled time, she would, she decided, put aside all the practical, logical reasons that nothing could ever come of an affair with Darius Wilde.

Sara was pragmatic enough to realize that regrets were inevitable; they might stay together for the duration of the tour, but once they reached sunny California, it would be time for Darius to return to the ivory towers of academia. Where, she hoped he would remember this summer as a magical interlude in never-never land.

"Show me," she insisted with an alluring laugh. She linked her fingers around his neck and coaxed him down on top of her. "Show me how special I am."

Sara's body was lean, supple and inviting as she rained scores of kisses over his face. Darius felt himself harden and marveled that he could be wanting her again so soon.

What was it about her? he wondered, as his lips willingly succumbed to the silky seduction of her mouth. She was beautiful, yes. But he had known other women just as lovely who hadn't had the power to make him burn. She was alive with unrestrained energy, yet he had certainly known other energetic women. And they had never made him tremble. She was intelligent, granted. But his world was full of intelligent women, none of whom had ever haunted his dreams night after lonely night.

While the scholarly, analytical part of his brain attempted to unravel the mystery of these tumultuous feelings for Sara, his emotional side was being seduced by her avid mouth, her slender hands. Then, as she opened for him, Darius forgot to think at all.

8

SARA AWOKE to the canarylike song of a goldfinch and the stirring aroma of fresh coffee brewing. Sitting up in the bunk, she stretched, working the kinks out of muscles that were unusually stiff this morning.

"If that's how you begin every day, I think I'll keep you around," Darius said as he approached the bunk with a cup of steaming coffee in each hand.

Sara smiled her thanks for both the coffee and the compliment. "I don't know that I'd want to stay," she murmured, taking a sip and finding it too hot to drink. "This bunk is terribly narrow; I don't think it was meant to sleep two."

"I wasn't talking about sleeping."

When his free hand trailed down the slope of her breast, Sara felt herself melting into the mattress. "We certainly didn't get much sleep last night," she said in a breathless little voice.

"Complaining?" His fingers were tracing warming circles around one dusky areola, and Darius smiled a satisfied smile as he watched her nipple harden in response.

"No." It was a whisper but easily heard in the glow of morning sunlight.

How could she want him again, after last night? Sara asked herself with a lingering sense of wonder. She'd lost count of the number of times they had turned to each other during the night, each time proving more thrilling, more satisfying than the last. Even as her body ached this morning, it remembered, growing moist under his increasingly seductive touch.

"How's the coffee?" he asked in a casual tone that was at odds with the building desire in his dark eyes.

"It's a little hot."

He nodded as he took the cup from her hand and deliberately placed it beside his on a nearby shelf. "Mine, too. I suppose, if we put our heads together, we could find something to do to kill time while it cools."

"The rain's stopped; we could take a walk," she suggested.

His gaze didn't leave hers. "That's one idea. We could also always play Scrabble."

"That's another," she agreed with a sharp intake of breath as his wickedly clever hand slipped under the sheet and unerring located the part of her body most aching for his touch. She leaned back against the pillow and closed her eyes, concentrating on his devastating touch.

"Or we could just try to drive each other crazy until it's time to go back for the afternoon performance."

As his thumb continued to brush tantalizingly against her, Sara climaxed. Warm, rippling waves flowed outward to her fingertips. "Oh, I vote for that one," she said with a laugh, reaching for him yet again.

"NOT ONLY WAS JEREMY a jerk, he was also a damn fool," Darius said later that morning.

After a long, lingering period of lovemaking, Sara and Darius had finally left the bed long enough to eat breakfast and get dressed. Now they were sitting contentedly on the grassy bank of the lake, watching a trio of ducks energetically diving for fish while a family of ring-necked pheasants fed in the underbrush nearby. An industrious tree swallow worked, diligently repairing an abandoned woodpecker's nest, while a family of robins played musical branches in the tree overhead.

Sara glanced over at him curiously. For some reason the thought or sound of her former husband's name no longer seemed to make her cringe. What a difference a single night could make, she realized wonderingly. Had it been the night? Or the man?

"What brought that up?"

He covered her hand with his. "The man was a jerk not to appreciate your many attributes," he said simply. "But he was a fool to let you get away."

Sara told herself that they were only words; they should not bring such pleasure. But they did. She smiled. "I'm glad he did."

Returning her smile, Darius lifted her hand to his lips. "Me, too. In fact, if I ever run into the guy, remind me to thank him."

"I doubt that you'll get the chance; when Jeremy left, he was headed back to England."

"England?"

"Oxford," she said weakly as his lips moved to the inside of her wrist. Her pulse pounded against the lingering kiss. A kiss that was threatening to make her forget everything except the havoc Darius was capable of wreaking on her body. "He was originally a tutor there; I met him when he was guest-lecturing at Penn."

"Aha. The reason for the prejudice concerning my occupation finally comes out."

Sara couldn't deny what they both knew to be the truth. "I've already admitted that I wasn't thrilled with Germaine's idea," she pointed out.

He slowly lowered their joined hands to his lap. "Yes, you have. But there's something important that you need to realize, sweetheart."

"What's that?"

His tone had suddenly turned gritty; his dark eyes, in the buttery rays of the morning sun, resembled chips of gleaming jet. "I'm not Jeremy. I'm nothing at all like that bastard."

His intense expression, after the bliss they had so recently shared, was making her extremely uncomfortable. "I know," she murmured.

"Do you?" His fingers cupped her chin, holding her eyes to his when she would have looked away. "Do you really, Sara?"

"Of course." His challenging tone succeeded in raising her ire, and she glared back at him. "Contrary to what some people may think about professional clowns, I'm not a mental midget, Darius. I'm perfectly capable of telling the difference between you and my former spouse."

He glared at her long and hard. "I certainly hope so," he said at length.

Despite the sunny warmth of the day, a cloud had settled over them. As they returned to the campground, neither seemed inclined toward lengthy conversation. Finally, deciding that the lingering silence was his fault for bringing up her damn ex-husband in the first place, Darius attempted to smooth things over.

"Why did you become a clown?"

"Because I couldn't play center field for the Phillies."

"No, really. I'd sincerely like to know."

"That really was one of the reasons," she insisted with a smile. Sara had never been one to hold a grudge, and she certainly didn't want to waste the remainder of what had begun as a beautiful day by sulking. "But the main reason was because I love clowning."

"I happen to like cheesecake, too," he pointed out. "But you don't see me applying at the Bellevue Stratford for the position of pastry chef."

"That's not the same. The circus allows me to express myself in ways I never imagined. Sometimes I look out into the audience and see people watching us with their mouths open; you've no idea what a thrill it is to be part of that."

"Where did you study?"

"I majored in theater at Sarah Lawrence. After that I studied clowning."

"Where?"

"The Ringling school, for one." She grinned. "It was Germaine's graduation present. She knew I'd dreamed of attending clown college for years."

"Funny, you don't remind me of any Ringling clown I've ever seen."

Her eyes narrowed. "Is that an insult? The Ringling Clown College just happens to be the best school of its kind in the country."

"It's the biggest," he countered easily. "You, of all people, should know that size doesn't always connote quality." His eyes gleamed with reminiscent warmth as they gave her a slow, seductive perusal.

"Some great clowns have come out of the Ringling school," Sara insisted.

"Granted. But most of them were naturally great before they arrived."

Her muttered sound could have been one of frustration or agreement.

"Let me make my point," he said. "What's the first thing you did when you got to Sarasota?"

"Pinched myself to make certain I wasn't dreaming."

"How about the second thing?"

"Unpacked my clothes."

Stubborn was one thing, impossible quite another. Darius ran a hand through his hair. "Let's fast-forward through this story until we get to the first class," he suggested dryly.

"All right; we learned to do our makeup."

"Whiteface."

"Yes." If her tone sounded defensive, it was because Sara could not determine where Darius was going with this particular line of questioning.

"Whiteface is a circus cliché," he countered. "A fact you obviously agree with, if the performance at the Peter and Wendy Circus are any indication."

"We have whiteface clowns," she challenged.

"Of course you do. But they're not your usual sentimental clichés. Instead, you employ more of a stylized technique. Along the lines of the European model."

"A few posters and the man's an expert," she grumbled, folding her arms over her chest as she glared at the verdant, sunlit fields.

"Am I wrong?"

"No," she agreed flatly. "You're not."

Sara was vaguely depressed to discover yet another thing she and Darius had in common. Each time she tried to convince herself that there was no future with this man, that their lives were light-years apart, he'd find yet another common denominator to chip away at her resolve.

"I'll admit to believing that the Ringling school does everything backward," she said slowly. "They have you selecting your makeup and costume before you even know who you are. That's what I've always believed clowning is all about—creating an utterly impossible, yet entirely plausible character. It's that paradox between the impossible and plausible that captures people's attention. Their imagination."

"I've always thought good clowning was merely creating an abstract of life," Darius offered. "In a way, clowns are the Kabuki theater of the circus."

Damn. He'd done it again.

"That's one of the reasons I wanted to profile your circus," he said when she remained silent. "Because it, more than any other I've ever seen, allows a performer to explore the theatrical side of clowning. The skits are like small plays in the ring—they give the same sort of feeling you get when watching a Buster Keaton or Charlie Chaplin movie."

That's precisely what they'd always tried to do, Sara acknowledged silently. Even back in the days when they were a small, ragtag group performing in the streets of Philadelphia, existing on little more than handouts from generous passersby.

"That's a very nice thing to say."

He shrugged. "It's true. I've always gotten the impression that the performers in the Peter and Wendy Circus and Penguin Extravaganza are actors first. And jugglers, tumblers and clowns second."

"You're very perceptive. I'm not the only member of the troupe to have a degree in drama. Several have performed on the stage. Donald West, for example, had the starring role in the opera *Orlando* at the Guthrie Theater in Minneapolis."

"I can see Don as a crusading knight," Darius allowed, thinking of the muscular tumbler.

"And Peter Longstreet was in *Biloxi Blues*, Jason Palmer's up for an understudy part in *Broadway Bound*, Diane Winters played the part of Elaine Harper in *Arsenic and Old Lace*, and Susan Murphy recently joined the troupe after appearing in repertory in a play called *Pravda* produced by the National Theater company in England."

"What about you?"

"Me?"

"Yes, you. What colorful performances do you have lurking in your checkered past?"

"Is this going to get into the book?" she asked suspiciously.

"Perhaps."

"Oh." Sara thought about that for a while. "I suppose it wouldn't damage my reputation," she mused. "All right, probably my best role was when I played the part of Kate in *The Taming of the Shrew*."

"Yet another case of typecasting," he murmured, chuckling when she shot him a withering glare. "Where? In Philadelphia?"

Sara professed a sudden overwhelming interest in the scenery flashing past the passenger window of the van. "No. It was off Broadway."

"I'm impressed."

She grinned, in spite of herself. "Don't be until you find out how far off," she advised.

"Idaho?"

She reached back and hit him lightly in the shoulder with her fist. "Not that far."

"Kansas?"

"You're getting warmer."

"Connecticut?"

"Bingo," she said with a laugh.

"All insults aside, you would make a great Kate," Darius said thoughtfully. "You've got an energy, a vitality, a love for life that would really come across to an audience. I'll bet you had a great time with the part."

"I loved it. It really was a fun production, Darius. The audience had a great time; I think you would have, too."

He reached out and ruffled her hair in a warm, familiar gesture. "I know I would have."

Over the past two weeks Darius had come to the conclusion that there was nothing about this half woman, half pixie, that he wouldn't find immensely enjoyable.

They shared a smile. The threatening cloud had been banished, leaving Sara and Darius free to bask in the mellow sunshine of the spring day and the radiant warmth of each other's company.

SOUTH DAKOTA WAS mile after uninterrupted mile of corn, wheat, barley and oats. It was crystal lakes formed by ancient glaciers and tall prairie grass waving languorously in the wind.

The performers had just concluded the last of two performances in Fort Pierre, when an oddly distracted Helga visited Sara's tent.

"It went well, don't you think?" she asked as she roamed nervously around the interior of the compact tent.

"Amazingly well," Sara agreed. "I still can't believe we got through the entire two and a half hours without anything going wrong." She grinned. "South Dakota must be our lucky state."

As if in need of something to do with her hands, Helga picked up a paperback Robert B. Parker novel and began flipping uninterestedly through the pages. "I wouldn't count on that if I were you," she advised. She put the book back onto the folding table and resumed her pacing.

The tall blond woman's surfeit of nervous energy reminded Sara of a caged panther. As she watched her friend's atypical behavior, she couldn't help thinking back to another time, only a few weeks ago, when she, not Helga, had been the one wearing a hole in the canvas floor.

"Would you please slow down enough to tell me what's wrong?"

Helga slumped into a canvas sling chair. "Oh, Sara, you're going to hate me."

"Never," Sara insisted promptly.

Helga's eyes were bleak as she observed her long-time friend and colleague. "This isn't my idea, you have to understand. It's Yuri's, and although I loathe the thought of any man telling me what I must do, I have to admit that he makes sense. Once he stops shouting, that is." She grimaced. "You know how dictatorial and chauvinistic he can be."

Sara's concern was escalating by the second. "Helga, this is not at all like you," she pressed anxiously. "Would you please just get to the point? Before I go stark, raving mad?"

"I've been doing my best to conceal my physical condition, but the fact is I can't perform any longer."

Sara's legs turned rubbery, and she knew that if she hadn't been sitting down, she would have fallen. "Oh, no," she whispered. "Oh, Helga, what is it?" Her whirling mind conjured up myriad possibilities, each more upsetting than the last.

"I'm going to have *ein Kindlein*."

"Ein Kindlein." It took Sara a moment to translate. "A baby? You're going to have a baby?"

Helga nodded. "Ja. I'm sorry."

"Sorry?" Sara jumped to her feet and put her arms around the other woman. "This is wonderful news! I know how long you and Yuri have been trying to have a baby."

"But the circus . . ."

Sara waved Helga's protest away. "For heaven's sake, don't even think about it; you're more important than the circus any day. A baby . . . You're so lucky."

"Ja. I know." Helga's soft, answering smile faded as her sober dark eyes settled on Sara's face. "I hope my news does not make you sad, Sara."

"Don't be silly. How could one of my best friends having a baby make me sad? It's wonderful news. I'm thrilled."

Helga returned Sara's hug. "I'm so glad." Her eyes misted with uncharacteristic moisture. "If the baby is a girl, we are going to call it Sara."

Sara laughed. "Not Natasha?"

"Natasha? Why should I name my sweet innocent child after that *Hexe*?"

"She may be a witch," Sara allowed, "but I seem to remember Yuri saying something about his mother anxiously awaiting a namesake."

Helga's short, pungent oath was in her native tongue, but Sara had no difficulty translating its meaning. "If that battle-ax of a mother-in-law desires a namesake, let her carry it for nine months. Otherwise, the child's name shall be Sara."

As pleased as Sara was, the last thing she wanted to do was cause a rift between Helga and her husband. "What does Yuri have to say about all this?"

"In some ways, it is a distinct advantage to be married to a man who refuses to accept the idea of women's liberation."

"Meaning he's so excited about the baby that he's willing to give you any little thing your heart desires?"

"*Ja.*" Helga's smug, womanly smile reminded Sara of the *Mona Lisa.* "Exactly."

IT WAS a little more than an hour later when Darius arrived at the tent to find Sara sitting alone in the dark. The grief had hit her unexpectedly. Now all she wanted was peace. And privacy while she struggled to deal with it.

"Sorry, I'm late," he said, making his way to the cooler and pulling out a beer. "The battery on the equipment truck was dead and we had to charge it. This is the second time the thing's died on us; I think you ought to consider buying a new one before heading out tomorrow morning. I'd hate to get stuck crossing the Badlands."

When Sara failed to answer, Darius lit the kerosene lantern. She immediately turned her head away, but not before he caught sight of the tear streaks staining her face.

"Sweetheart—what's wrong?"

She shook her head, refusing to meet his concerned gaze. When she heard him moving toward her, she held up her hand. "Please," she whispered. "Just go. I really need to be alone right now."

"I'm afraid I can't do that."

"Why not?"

"Because I care about you," he answered simply. "And because it's obvious that you're hurting."

His empathetic, considerate tone pulled at something deep within her, causing Sara to swallow a sob. "This is personal, Darius," she insisted softly. "It doesn't have anything to do with you."

"Doesn't it?"

She shook her head viciously. "No. It's my problem; I'll deal with it in my own way."

Refusing to stay away from her any longer, Darius went over and sat on the arm of the overstuffed chair. "If sitting all alone in the dark and crying is your way of dealing with a problem, perhaps you need some help."

"You are so insufferably egotistical," she flared, looking at him for the first time since he'd entered the tent. "What makes you possibly think I'd need your help?"

He put his arm around her shoulders. The summer night was warm; Sara's slender body was like ice. "I ran into Helga earlier," he said conversationally, even as anxiety was battering his insides to a pulp. "She said you might want to talk to me; if I'd known you were so upset, I would have said the hell with the battery and come right over."

Sara jerked, as if to pull away, but Darius's arm tightened. "She had no right to involve you." When he didn't answer, Sara took a deep, shuddering breath. "Helga's pregnant."

"I know."

"You do?"

"Yuri told me right before the evening performance; the guy is floating on air. Right now he could probably reach that tightrope without a ladder." His fingers stroked the top of her arm. "Is something wrong with Helga? Is that why you're so upset?"

Sara pressed her hands against her temples and took a deep breath, which she let out in a slow, shuddering sigh. "Helga's fine."

Still unable to discern what was tearing Sara in two, he gathered her to him. "But you're not," he murmured, resting his chin on her head. "You know, sweetheart, sometimes it helps to talk things out."

She made one last halfhearted attempt to break free of his gentle hold before giving herself up to the warmth and comfort offered by his strong arms. "Oh, God, it hurts," she moaned, shutting her eyes. "After all this time it still hurts." Sara dabbed at the fresh moisture stinging her eyes.

"I know, love," Darius murmured, not really knowing anything at all but wanting to offer what scant comfort he could. "I know." He rocked her in his arms, murmuring soft, consoling words as he brushed away the tears streaming down her face.

Unable to hold in her feelings any longer, Sara allowed them to break free. Grief. Guilt. Regrets. Emotions flooded from her heart, her soul, like a torrent bursting through the walls of a dam. Powerless against the tide, Sara clung to him, sobbing into the hard line of his shoulder.

After an immeasurable time Darius could tell by her slow, steady breathing that Sara's overwhelming grief had run its course. "Feel better?" he asked, brushing his lips against her forehead.

"I think so." She pressed her palm experimentally against her chest, as if checking to see if her heart were still broken.

"But it still hurts."

Sara looked up at him. "Yes," she admitted in a whisper. "But I suppose I should be used to that by now."

The lingering pain in her misty eyes succeeded in tearing his own heart to pieces. Darius felt himself imbued with a tenderness he'd never before experienced. And with that tenderness, he realized, came love. Even as he acknowledged the emotion, he wondered how it was he had not recognized it before this. He was so caught up in the wonder of it that he almost missed her next words.

"I had a child," she whispered raggedly.

A fist twisted his insides in two. "With Jeremy," he managed.

She nodded. Slowly. Painfully. "With Jeremy," she agreed, even as her former husband's name threatened to choke her. "Her name was Amy. She had big blue eyes and the softest skin. It was like pink satin. And whenever she smiled at me, I felt as if the sun had suddenly come from behind a dark cloud."

"I know the feeling," Darius murmured. "Very well."

"Oh, Darius, I loved her so very, very much."

A lone tear slid down her cheek; he brushed it away with a fingertip. "I know you did."

"When she was six weeks old, the theater group was invited to perform at the governor's inaugural ball. It meant more publicity than we'd ever dreamed of receiving. Naturally, I was ecstatic."

"Naturally."

"We'd all worked so hard, yet we always seemed to be drowning in a sea of red ink. I thought this was the perfect opportunity to acquire additional funding. I mean, once everyone saw how good we were, how professional—"

"Sara," Darius interrupted, "you don't have to convince me that performing at the ball was a golden opportunity. I can see how it would have been."

Her blue eyes searched his. "Can you? Can you really?"

"Of course." Something occurred to him. "Jeremy was less than enthusiastic about the prospect, wasn't he?"

Her slender shoulders slumped dejectedly. "He hated the idea."

"But why?" Darius was honestly confused. "Surely he was proud of your accomplishments."

She laughed, but the flat sound carried no mirth. "The only accomplishments Jeremy considered worth discussing were his own scholarly pursuits. My rather unique successes, on the other hand, he viewed as nothing short of an embarrassment."

Personally, from what he'd been able to discern of Sara's former husband, Darius felt that she was way off the mark with that one but decided to keep his views to himself for the time being. There was nothing to be gained by upsetting her further with unnecessary arguments.

"Anyway," she said with a soft, rippling little sigh of regret when Darius remained silent, "Jeremy called while I was getting ready to leave; something had come up at the university, something that required his attention. So he couldn't stay home with Amy."

Couldn't? Darius wondered bitterly. Or wouldn't?

"I called Mrs. Konklin, from upstairs," Sara continued flatly. "She'd sat with the baby before, Amy knew her. And liked her." She drew in a deep, shuddering breath. "I thought it would be all right."

As her eyes filled once more with hot, anguished tears, Darius felt as if he were drowning. "Sweetheart, if this is too difficult, you don't have to—"

"No." Her nails dug into her palms. "I want to tell you; it's important that you know." She swallowed, struggling to talk past the enormous lump in her throat. "The show was a smashing success; the applause seemed to go on forever. We were all in seventh heaven. I don't remember driving home; I think I probably flew."

She was trembling like a wounded sparrow. As he tightened his arms around her, Darius was reminded once again how slender Sara was. How delicate. How vulnerable.

He kissed the top of her head. "I wish I'd been there to see it."

Sara wrapped her arms around him and pressed her cheek against his chest. "I wish you had been." She let out another deep, shuddering breath as she garnered her strength to continue. Sara didn't understand why it was suddenly so important that Darius know her guilty secret. She only knew that she must tell him.

"I got home a little after eleven o'clock. Mrs. Konklin was watching an old movie on television. It was a Bette Davis movie," she said irrelevantly. "The one where she plays a spoiled Southern belle who wears a flaming red dress to a debutante ball."

"*Jezebel*," he murmured against her hair.

Sara nodded. "That's it. I remember because I sat down for a few minutes to watch the ending with her." In truth, it would have been impossible for Sara to have forgotten anything about that night. The events had been seared into her mind.

"Where was Jeremy?"

"Still at the university, I suppose. I paid Mrs. Konklin; I was out of cash so I had to write her a check. Unfortunately I couldn't remember where I'd left my checkbook. Oh, she assured me I could simply pay her the next day, but for some reason I just kept searching for that damn checkbook. I finally found it in the kitchen junk drawer."

Her voice had gone strangely flat, and her eyes had glazed over once again with a dull pain. His nerves were all on edge, and he was afflicted with a sense of impending doom, as if he'd suddenly found himself in the middle of a Stephen King novel. It took every ounce of self-restraint Darius possessed to keep from urging her to hurry the story along.

She was staring straight ahead, but Darius knew Sara was not seeing the olive-drab tent flap. From her unnatural pallor he could tell she was reliving that long-ago night. "After Mrs. Konklin went back upstairs, I went into the nursery to check Amy."

She closed her eyes tightly. The scene continued to play behind her lids as it had done every night for months after the tragedy. Opening her eyes, she continued. "I'd given her a bath before going out. And dressed her in a fuzzy sleeper. The kind with the feet. She was forever kicking off her blankets, so I'd bought it to keep her feet warm. It was white. With little yellow ducks printed all over it."

A sound perilously close to a sob escaped her. "Her tiny thumb was stuck between her little rosebud lips. She looked so peaceful. So still." She swallowed a tremor as the pain, dark and insidious, slipped through her defences. "Oh, God. Amy." Her mouth tried to form the words to tell Darius exactly what had happened, but nothing came out.

Darius could guess the rest. He remained silent and waited, understanding that Sara needed to tell this in her own way. At her own pace.

"At first I thought she was asleep. Then I could see that she wasn't breathing. I screamed for Mrs. Konklin; she came right away and called the paramedics while I gave Amy mouth-to-mouth resuscitation, but even though they didn't stop working on her until after we'd gotten to the hospital, I knew that it was too late.

"I tried to call Jeremy from the hospital, but he wasn't answering his office phone. Apparently he arrived home shortly after the ambulance left; Mrs. Konklin told him what had happened. The minute he walked into the emergency waiting room, I could tell that the marriage was over. I'd lost my baby and my husband, all in one night. A night that only a few hours earlier had been one of the happiest of my life."

Sara felt the tears rising behind her lids again and squeezed her eyes shut. "The doctor on duty diagnosed it as Sudden Infant Death Syndrome," she whispered haltingly. "He was a nice, grandfatherly type of man, with a soft, gentle voice and the kindest, saddest eyes. I vaguely remember feeling sorry for him, surrounded by so much death, so much suffering."

Darius heard the pain in her ragged voice, saw it in her eyes and tried to think of something to say that could make the anguish go away. In lieu of any such words, he held her.

"He tried to tell me that there had been no way of knowing ahead of time that Amy was susceptible to SIDS, that there was nothing I could have done. Nothing that anyone could have done."

She dragged a visibly trembling hand through her hair. "But I knew that if only I'd stayed home that night, if only I hadn't sat down to watch the end of the movie, if only I hadn't insisted on finding my checkbook, or if I hadn't lost it in the first place, Amy would still be alive. Jeremy didn't return home with me. I wasn't surprised; he hadn't said a single word to me the entire time we were waiting for the doctor to come out from behind those closed doors. The next day he sent a friend— a colleague from the university—over to the apartment to pick up his things. Two weeks later he filed for divorce. I never saw him again. I don't think he ever forgave me."

Darius had the distinct impression that the real problem was that Sara had never forgiven herself. He cupped her distressed face in his hand. Her eyes were puffy, red rimmed from crying. Another rogue tear escaped, sliding down her cheek like a silver ribbon; he kissed it away.

Darius vowed that if he ever had an opportunity to repay Jeremy McBride for even a portion of the unnecessary grief he'd caused Sara, he wouldn't hesitate. He couldn't remember ever being so furious, and although it took a major effort, he managed to remind himself that what Sara needed now was not uncontrolled masculine rage but soft words and gentle touches. Darius did his best to give them to her.

"Sweetheart, that is a horribly tragic story, granted. But there was nothing to forgive."

"I should have been there," she said numbly.

The dull pain in her voice made his temper flare again. He struggled to control it. For her sake. "The doctor was right. It wouldn't have mattered."

"But—"

Frustrated by his inability to reach her and rattled by almost overwhelming feelings of tenderness, Darius wanted to take Sara by the shoulders and shake some sense into her. Instead, he forced his hand to relax as he smoothed the hair away from her tear-streaked face. "Sara, it wasn't your fault. It wasn't anyone's fault. You can't live the rest of your life wondering about *what ifs*, sweetheart. It's time to let it rest."

Sara took a long, deep breath and appeared momentarily soothed by it. "I want to. Oh, God, how I want to."

"That's a start."

He kissed her face where the salty tears were still drying. As a surge of staggering emotion coursed through him, Darius wondered how he had managed to survive for this long without Sara McBride in his life. And although he wanted nothing more than to share the amazing news of his newfound love with her, instinct told him that she'd had enough emotional surprises for one day. For now he'd have to be content with merely demonstrating the extent of his feelings.

But with a certainty that was as surprising as it was intense, Darius vowed that when they returned to Philadelphia after the tour had come to an end, her whimsical dancing bear would be sitting on the shelf right beside his Mayan fertility fetish. Where it belonged. And Sara would be spending all her nights in his arms. Where she belonged.

As his mouth covered hers, Sara felt something warm and wonderfully alive shimmering through her, like rippling waves of golden sunshine. She clung to him, allowing the searing heat to burn away the lingering pain.

9

IF SOUTH DAKOTA WAS miles of uninterrupted prairie, it was also the Badlands—an eerily beautiful, disturbing land, full of strange and scalded shapes. Shapes that had been carved by a one-hundred-and-twenty-million-year history during which a great sea had come and gone and mountains had risen, only to crumble back to earth.

As they traveled through the state, a strong, steady wind from the west caused the yellowing grass to tremble. The land turned parched, dry and incredibly empty. The prairie became broken and blemished by low outcroppings of bare, beige rock.

It was there that they stopped for a performance on the Pine Ridge Indian Reservation during what their apologetic hosts explained was a record-breaking heat wave.

Sara hadn't needed the weather bulletin; she'd been fantasizing about a swimming pool filled to the rim with ice cubes ever since they'd begun setting up shop. More than once she'd looked out over the shimmering landscape and imagined a brilliant forest, as far as the eye could see, made up of tall, icy grape and banana and cherry Popsicles.

It could have been inattention, due to the oppressive heat. Or it could have simply been an unavoidable accident. Whatever, Orrin Adams, a twenty-one-year-old juggler with a brand-new degree in philosophy from Oberlin College, slipped on the rigging while setting up the overhead lights and fell to the sawdust below. Although his injuries were limited to a sprained ankle and assorted cuts and bruises, it was obvious that he was not going to be able to perform for several days.

After seeing that he was comfortable, or as comfortable as anyone could be with a sprained ankle in the oppressive, one-hundred-degree heat, Sara went off in search of Darius.

"There you are," she said with a smile when she found him unloading wooden bleachers from the equipment truck. "I've been looking all over for you."

"I've been right here." He grinned his appreciation as he accepted the soft drink she offered and downed it in a few thirsty swallows. "What's up?"

Sara retrieved the empty can, pressing the still-cool aluminum against her forehead. It was so hot. "There's been an accident."

Darius was instantly alert. "An accident? Who? Where? Was anyone hurt?"

"It's Orrin. He fell while stringing the lights."

"Damn." Darius liked the bright, enthusiastic young man. Before he'd begun spending most of his time with Sara, Darius had enjoyed philosophical discussions with him that had often gone on long into the night. "How badly is he hurt?"

"He was lucky; it's only a sprained ankle. But it does leave us short a valuable performer."

He had seen that look in her eyes before. It was a gleam that appeared whenever Sara was about to coax someone into doing something they were dead set against doing. He'd witnessed it for the first time when she was stopped for speeding outside Des Moines. Darius had not been at all surprised when the patrolman not only refrained from giving her a ticket, but also asked for her autograph, "for his kids."

That same gleam had been in evidence when she'd talked Gunner Knutson, a retired Army mess sergeant they met after a performance in Sioux City, into joining the troupe as a full-time company cook, the first the circus had ever had.

"Don't expect me to replace Orrin; I don't know how to juggle," he reminded her now.

Sara patted his cheek. "Now, Darius, don't be so hard on yourself. Don't forget, I watched you last night at dinner. Why, everyone is marveling at how proficient you've become in only a month."

"Tossing two apples and one orange in the air does not make me a professional juggler. Besides, in case you weren't paying close attention, sweetheart, I dropped them as often as I managed to catch them."

"I always pay attention to you, darling," she assured him blithely. "And don't worry, you'll improve. You simply need to develop the mind of a juggler."

"The mind of a juggler?" he questioned dubiously.

"It's a bit like meditation: you have to think of everything as being in the air, everything as being catchable. You know, give and take. Ebb and flow. Yin and yang. Once you start thinking that way, you'll be juggling seven balls in no time. Without even thinking about it."

"Somehow I doubt that. But even so, surely even a cockeyed optimist like you can realize that I'm not ready to juggle in front of an audience."

"Well, of course you're not," she agreed instantly. "I certainly wouldn't think of asking you to do anything like that." her smooth brow furrowed. "Cockeyed?"

"It was merely a figurative expression. Your eyes, as you damn well know, are exceptionally lovely."

Sara nodded. "Thank you. That's much better. Cockeyed," she muttered under her breath.

Darius was still waiting to discern the reason behind that unmistakable gleam. "If you're not here to con me into making a fool of myself by dropping fruit in front of a crowd of total strangers, what nefarious scheme do you happen to have up your sleeve this time?"

"Up my sleeve?" she repeated with wide, innocent eyes as she held out her bare arms. "Why, nothing at all. See?"

If there was one time Darius had learned not to trust Sara, it was when her lovely face took on that guileless, butter-wouldn't-melt-in-her-mouth expression.

"Well," he said, "since you seem to have everything under control, I guess I'd better get back to work." He turned away and began pulling a long painted plank from the back of the truck.

"Well, there is just one little thing."

Darius put the board on the ground with the others, then slowly straightened. "Funny. I thought there just might be."

"We can survive without Orrin's juggling act for one or two nights," she said quickly, as if she wanted to get the words out all at once before he could find reason to object. "Although it is definitely one of the major highlights of the show. Why, do you know, the first time I saw him juggling that enormous ax, sledgehammer and flaming baton, all at the same time, I thought—"

"Sara. Why don't you just get to the point," Darius suggested.

"Oh. Yes. Well." She took a deep breath. "It's the finale."

"No."

Her blue eyes turned as clear as a cloudless summer sky. "Darius, please."

"I said no." He stuck his hands in his back pockets and silently vowed to hold firm. "I will not, under any circumstances, let you put me into one of those damn penguin suits."

"But we can't do the finale without you."

"Why not? You already have eleven other people who don't mind making idiots of themselves. Besides, do you have any idea how hot it will be in one of those suits today?"

"Of course I do, since I'm going to be in one of them," she acknowledged. "And the fact that we only have eleven people is precisely the point, Darius. The penguin tap dance number is choreographed for an even dozen."

"So change the choreography."

"We can't. Not at this short notice. Eleven isn't an even number."

As he felt himself giving in, Darius stiffened his spine, as well as his resolve. "So cut one penguin and do the dance with ten."

"That would be false advertising."

He raised a brow challengingly. "I fail to see the connection."

"You can't possibly stage a penguin extravaganza with only ten penguins; it's hard enough with twelve. Helga had to work for months to make the dance number look like one of those old-time thirties' musical numbers. It's our trademark, Darius. Our theme song. She'd be absolutely heartbroken if we had to pull it from the program."

Sara lowered her head, kicking at the parched ground with the toe of her ragged sneaker. "So would I."

He let out a low, pungent oath. "I can't tap-dance. Or has that little detail slipped your mind?"

"Don't worry, you'll be in the chorus line," she assured him enthusiastically, meeting his frown with a dazzling smile. "Helga can teach you all the steps you need to know in an hour."

"I know I'm going to regret this."

"But you'll do it?"

"I'll do it."

From his dark glower, Sara decided that it would not be prudent to flaunt her victory. Instead, she flung her arms around his neck and gave him a hug. "Thank you, darling. I knew you wouldn't let us down."

"Why don't you wait to thank me until after the show," he suggested dryly as his arms went around her waist. Her enticing scent surrounded them, soothing his exasperation. "For all you know, I'm going to screw up the famed finale of the Peter and Wendy Family Circus and Penguin Extravaganza."

"Oh, you'll be fine," she insisted, tilting her head back to smile up at him. "Better than fine. You'll be terrific. And believe me, the finale is a lot of fun. Just wait and see, Darius, I promise that you'll have an absolutely marvelous time."

"The marvelous time will come later. After the performance. When we go to bed and you reward me for my unselfish, show-must-go-on contribution."

This time her smiling eyes held myriad sensual promises. "Oh, that's the very least that I can do." She kissed him quickly before breaking away.

"Don't worry about those bleachers; I'll send someone else to take care of them," she said as she jogged backward toward the spot where three members of the group were setting up the center ring. "You'd better get going; Helga's waiting for you."

With that she was gone, leaving Darius to wonder, not for the first time since meeting Sara McBride, exactly what he'd gotten himself into.

As THE HALCYON MONTH of June gave way to July and July to August, Sara felt as if the bright, sunny days were trying to outdo each other. Every day seemed a celebration as she basked in the glow of Darius's company. Every night brought pleasures that she had never imagined, even in her most romantic of fantasies.

And if every mile brought them nearer to the end of the tour, to the time when she and Darius returned to their own beds, their own lives, Sara wouldn't allow herself to dwell on that unhappy, if ultimately inevitable fact. She had always believed in living life one day at a time.

At the moment those days were more wonderful than anything she had ever known. And when they came to an end in California, she would allow herself one— perhaps two—days of mourning. All right, she admitted, maybe a week. But then she would get on with her life. As she always had in the past. And would continue to do in the future.

"What's the inflationary price of a thought these days?" he asked as they drove across Wyoming's desolate range country.

There were no highway lights, no cities glowing in the distance. Radio stations were drifting in and out like fleetingly overheard conversations at a cocktail party.

"Hmm?"

"You've been awfully quiet."

Sara continued to look out at the starry sky. She wasn't about to reveal that she'd been giving in to an uncharacteristic bout of self-pity. "Sorry."

He reached out and took her hand, linking their fingers. "You don't have to apologize; it's just that it's not like you not to be talking a hundred miles a minute. I was worried that you might not be feeling well."

His gentle concern only succeeded in making her feel all the more miserable. Whatever was she going to do when he'd gone? "I'm feeling fine."

He glanced over at her, his expression, in the slanting moonlight, unmistakably worried. Although neither of them had brought the subject up again, ever since she'd told him the story of her child, Darius had found himself constantly taking her emotional temperature, seeking signs of distress. He knew he was probably being overly cautious, but he couldn't seem to help himself. "Are you sure?"

Shaking off the melancholia that had settled over her like a heavy cape, Sara gave him a reassuring, although somewhat forced, smile. "Positive." The radio had faded to an irritating crackle. Sara reached out and twisted the dial, silencing it for good.

"Someone should put together a collection of traveling songs and record them," she said, wanting nothing more than to change the subject before she embarrassed them both by beginning to cry.

"Perhaps you should think about making that your off-season project."

She chewed thoughtfully on a thumbnail as she put away her dreary thoughts and considered his suggestion. "That's not such a bad idea, Darius. In fact, it's a marvelous idea. Just think of all the money it would bring in.... Truckers," she said suddenly.

"Truckers?" He glanced up at the rearview mirror, seeing only the yellow headlights of Yuri and Helga's motor home.

"I'll bet long-haul truckers would snap the tapes up like hotcakes. After all, who spends more time on the road than they do?"

"No one," he agreed. "You'd undoubtedly have to include Willie Nelson's 'On the Road Again.'"

"Of course. And Springsteen's 'Drive All Night.'"

"I can certainly identify with that one. Springsteen also recorded 'Badlands,'" he reminded her.

"We could have played that back in South Dakota," she agreed, warming up to the idea. Never one to dwell on the negative, Sara vowed not to think about the end of the summer any more than was necessary.

"'Route 66' is a classic," he said.

"Granted. And don't forget about 'This Land is Your Land.'"

"'By the Time I Get to Phoenix.'"

"'King of the Road.'"

There was a long silence as they tried to come up with yet another appropriate song title. "'Alabamy Bound,'" Darius challenged.

"'Mahogany,'" she continued.

"That's not a road song."

"Of course it is," Sara insisted. "'Do you know where you're going to?'" she sang the opening line of the romantic ballad slightly off-key.

"You realize, of course, that you're cheating with that one."

Sara nodded. "Of course."

"And I suppose you expect me to let you count it so you can win."

"I'd be very grateful."

"We'll be in Jackson Hole in another hour," he announced significantly as he glanced down at the dashboard clock. "Prepare to be very, very grateful."

"Does that mean I win?"

The light touch of her hand on his thigh combined with her slow smile caused desire to slam into him. It was all Darius could do not to pull over to the side of the road and take her here. Now.

Just one more hour until his carefully planned surprise. *Sixty short minutes*, he assured his aching body. *Thirty-six hundred agonizingly long seconds.* He didn't know how he was going to survive the wait.

"Don't you always?" he asked.

His attention was directed out the windshield, but Sara had no difficulty discerning the slight deepening of his voice and knew that he wanted to make love to her. Not that he was alone in that desire. Her body was warming now, just thinking about it.

Sara had always believed in following her instincts. But lately she had begun to be frightened by the way her feelings had of spiraling out of control, of taking her to dizzying heights she never had believed existed. The fear was, of course, that these same emotions might also drag her down into the very depths of despair.

The way Darius could make her want him with unrestrained passion was unnerving. That she thought about him almost every waking minute was unsettling. And that she could no longer imagine a life without him was terrifying.

"I think," she said slowly, "that most of the time we both win."

Darius heard the faint hesitation in her tone and wondered briefly at the cause. "Every time," he confirmed, pressing down on the accelerator.

"WHAT ARE YOU DOING?" Sara asked as Darius pulled up in front of the lodge at Jackson Hole.

He twisted the key, turning off the ignition. "Getting us a room."

"But—"

Leaning over, he planted a quick, hard kiss on her frowning lips. "Humor me," he said quietly. "I want to sit across the table from you in a real restaurant and watch the candlelight dance in your hair. I want to share a shower with you that isn't shoved into a damn broom closet. And most of all," he said, running a hand down her hair, "I want to sleep with you in a real bed. A wide, soft one, with fat, fluffy pillows and a down comforter."

How could such an innocent touch make her heart pound? "Do you actually expect me to believe that you intend to sleep on this wide, soft bed?"

"Of course." His lips caressed hers enticingly. "After we make love, of course."

Sara tasted the urgency on his lips and felt it echo deep inside her. "Professor, I do like your style."

His eyes, as they looked into hers, were calm and confident. "Believe me, woman, you haven't seen anything yet."

"HOW LONG ARE YOU planning to stay in there?" Darius asked thirty minutes later. He was leaning against the doorjamb of the bathroom, watching the enticing shadow behind the vinyl shower curtain.

Sara closed her eyes and tilted her head back, allowing the warm water to sluice over her. "Forever. Do you realize what a marvelous thing it is not to worry about using up all the hot water?"

"I seem to remember a time, not so very long ago, when I didn't worry about such things." Not so long ago? It could have been in another lifetime. Darius suddenly realized that as long as he lived, he would only be able to think of time as being either Before Sara or After Sara.

"Has it been that rough?" She unwrapped a bar of soap and began lathering her body.

Unable to resist the inviting shadows, Darius took off his clothes, pulled the curtain back and joined her in the blue-and-white tiled shower. "Not at all." Plucking the soap from her hands, he took over the job. "Besides, this trip comes with dynamite benefits."

When his soapy hands began caressing her breasts, Sara felt a swirl of sensation that almost made her knees buckle. Tingling vibrations ran from her nipples to her sex.

"Darius..."

"Yes, sweetheart?" The soap slid slickly down her slender body. His fingers tangled in the fiery curls at the juncture of her thighs, drawing a ragged moan from her lips.

"Darius, don't. I want to stop now."

"But I thought you planned to stay in here all night." His hand slipped between her legs.

"That was earlier." Sara grasped his broad shoulders to keep from falling. "Before you began making me crazy."

His fingers slipped into her. "Do I make you crazy, Sara?"

"Damn you." It was a half moan, half laugh. "You know you do."

"Mmm." His thumb tantalizingly stroked her petaled softness as he appeared to be considering her words. "I think I like knowing I can make you crazy."

His increasingly intimate touch was driving her insane. A slow, spiraling warmth was spreading outward from her innermost core. Sara's nails dug into his skin. "Watch it," she warned on a trembling breath, "your ego's showing again."

He smiled. "I know." His lips covered hers in a deep, drugging kiss. "Disgusting, isn't it?" Then he touched her—really touched her—and Sara crested in a series of steep, shuddering peaks.

When she returned to earth, she was drifting on warm, sensuous waves. Her body remained warm and deliciously languid as she allowed Darius to rub her dry with a fluffy white bath towel, and when he lifted her into his arms, she felt as if she were floating.

Sara's dreamy lassitude disintegrated the moment he carried her into the adjoining bedroom. The room was bathed in the warm, flickering light of sparkling white candles. A bottle of champagne was nestled in a silver bucket, surrounded by a crystal bed of ice. Two tall fluted glasses waited nearby.

White roses bloomed everywhere: on the dresser, on the seat of the ladder-back chair beside the door, on the floor surrounding the bed. Rose petals had been scattered over the peach satin sheets, looking like snowflakes in the muted, glowing light.

"You planned this," she accused in a stunned whisper as Darius placed her on the bed. The sweet scent of the roses swirled in her head, and the velvety petals caressed her freshly bathed skin.

"Guilty."

He lay down beside her and kissed her ears, her eyelids, her hair. Billie Holiday was singing softly in the background. "I've been going crazy for the last hundred miles thinking about this."

The tantalizing kisses moved down her throat, skimming along her collarbone. "Thinking about your taste." His tongue traced the outline of her parted lips before slipping inside. "The satin of your skin." His wide dark hand caressed her from shoulder to thigh, setting her on fire once again.

In a sudden change of mood Sara slipped out of his light embrace, going up on her knees. Her wet hair tumbled carelessly over her shoulders to touch the curve of her breasts.

"Were you really going crazy?" she asked, brushing her smiling lips against his.

"You know I was."

Sara laughed lightly. Her breath warmed his lips, but when he put his hand at the back of her head to pull her down to him, she pulled away.

"No," she insisted. "Not yet."

Her hands flitted down his chest, her fingers toying with the dark curls. "They're so soft," she murmured, stroking him with a tantalizingly light touch. "Like thistledown." She rubbed her cheeks against them. Darius imagined he could hear her purr. "From the way they look, you'd expect them to be stiff. Springy." Her tongue cut a slow, moist swathe through the ebony hairs. "But they're not at all, are they?"

His body was beginning to burn with an escalating, impatient urgency. Because he was accustomed to always being in control of every aspect of his life, it was coming as a shock to Darius that what he was currently feeling was nothing less then pure helplessness.

"What in God's name do you think you are doing?" he managed to croak out as her hand trailed idly up his thigh, managing to feather the hair without touching his heated skin.

"Turnabout's fair play, Darius. I want to know." She nipped lightly at his shoulder. A soft sheen of perspiration glistened on his skin; Sara sighed as she reveled in the sharp, salty taste. "No, I take that back. I *need* to know."

The weeks of working in the sun had left his body hard and tanned to the rich, deep color of mahogany. Sara touched him everywhere, loving the feel of his taut, lean muscles as they leaped and rippled under her wandering hand. She took her time, discovering how the brush of a fingernail against his dark nipple inflamed, the caress of her lips against his belly aroused.

"Know what?" he managed as thunder roared in his ears. "You can turn me to jelly."

"Definitely not jelly." Her sultry laugh shimmered across his moist flesh as her lips brushed over his hips. Sara reveled in the taste of him and knew that she'd never get her fill. "I want to know that I can drive you as crazy as you've been making me all these weeks."

Her hair trailed wetly over Darius as her open lips left flaming paths over his torso. Her warmth passed into him and he groaned. She moved her body sinuously against his, like a sleek cat, and he burned. Finally, unable to take the tender torment any longer, Darius gripped her waist as he lifted her over him.

"I want you," he said as flames licked dangerously at his blood. "Now."

Her head was tilted back, her long hair cascading down her back like a coppery waterfall. Her eyes were glowing, but there was nothing that remotely resembled submission in their gleaming depths. She looked wild. And wanton. Darius knew that if she had looked this way back in the days of witch-hunts, she would have been burned at the stake.

"Tell me," Sara insisted, her relentless gaze burning into his, fire meeting fire. "Tell me how much you want me."

"Can't you see?" he challenged roughly. "Even now?" His fingers tightened. "You're my insanity." When their lips met, Darius drew in the mingling of their tastes and thought he would explode.

Sara's head was spinning as she drew him inside her. There was a jolt of almost intolerable pleasure. Then, as the world shattered into a million glittering fragments, both knew that nothing would ever be the same again.

10

SARA HAD ARRANGED the schedule so that the troupe had seven long and luxurious days in Wyoming. After all the long, hot weeks on the road, it was nice to have some time to take a well-deserved breather in the shade of the Grand Teton's craggy peaks. She'd been coming to Wyoming for four years, and every time she found herself contrasting the village of Jackson with the quaint mountain towns of Vermont and New Hampshire or the tidy, Alpine villages of Switzerland.

Sara and Darius took long walks, sat by the banks of crystal creeks, ate, slept, laughed and made love. It was a time apart; a time in which they learned to enjoy each other's company without the hectic pace the circus had entailed.

If they talked of nothing important, it was by mutual, unspoken consent. If they failed to discuss the future, it was due to Sara's vow to think only of one blissful, sun-kissed day at a time. Darius was finding it more and more difficult to withhold his feelings, but he sensed Sara's reluctance to commit herself to a long-term relationship.

Although he certainly didn't agree with her seemingly free and easy attitude, California—and the end of the tour—was still two weeks away. And while he was rapidly discovering an impatience he'd never known he possessed, Darius was willing to give Sara a bit more time to get used to the idea of spending the rest of their lives together.

Besides, he thought on more than one occasion, in a few days they'd be returning to Philadelphia for Germaine's party. Though at first he'd been irritated by the woman's meddling in his life, he was ready to admit that he wouldn't complain if their mutual friend gave Sara a gentle shove toward commitment.

There were times during the brief vacation that Sara found Darius slightly more quiet, more introspective than usual, and she'd begin to worry that he was growing bored, or restless. It was then that his thoughtful silence would grate on her nerves until she wanted to scream.

But she didn't. All too aware that their affair was coming to an end, Sara didn't want to waste time arguing. It was better not to think about it, she told herself one day as they walked hand in hand along the banks of Jackson Lake. Not now. Not when she was experiencing a pleasure she'd never known existed.

"You're awfully quiet this afternoon." Darius's low voice broke into her studied concentration.

"So are you."

"Ah, but I haven't been frowning for the past hour."

"I haven't been frowning."

His fingers brushed lightly at the furrowed skin of her forehead. "Yes, you have. And it makes me wonder if I've done something to displease you."

"Never," she said instantly. Her smile was quick, bright and entirely false.

It was not the first time he'd watched her struggle in vain to hide her tumultuous feelings. He couldn't help wondering if the absent Jeremy McBride had been fool enough to attempt a smooth ride with his young wife and decided, from Sara's increasingly frequent efforts to please, that he had. Personally, Darius had preferred it when she'd allowed her emotions more freedom.

Until meeting Sara, Darius had always managed to keep his life in nice, tidy little pockets. His adventures had been limited to his work, to his anthropological expeditions that took him all over the world, seeking to discover ways that cultures had changed under the influence of modern civilization.

When it came to his relationships with women, Darius had always preferred predictable, mutually undemanding affairs with women he'd met at the various universities he'd settled at for a brief spell before moving on. During his days with the Peter and Wendy Family Circus and Penguin Extravaganza, Darius had come to realize exactly how restless he'd been, traveling the globe, searching for something that always remained just out of reach.

At least it had until Sara. Oh, he knew that a life with Sara McBride would never be smooth or predictable. But it would also never be boring.

She was pretending a sudden interest in the shimmering clouds garlanding the jagged ridge of the Tetons. A summer storm was coming; she could feel the electricity humming just under her skin. Or perhaps, Sara considered, as she felt his grave dark eyes directed at her face, it was his increasingly intense study that had her feeling so jumpy.

He took her face in his hands. "You don't have to pretend with me, Sara. Ever."

Why had she ever thought she could hide anything from this man? "I've been thinking about Helga," she said, not entirely untruthfully.

It was not the answer he'd been expecting. "Helga?"

"Does she look a little pale to you lately?"

"No. But I suppose that's to be expected, considering her condition. Besides, sweetheart, you know that the only woman I ever notice around here is you."

The words shouldn't have had the ability to please her so very, very much. But they did. "I suppose I'm expected to believe that you didn't notice that reporter hanging all over you in South Dakota."

"What reporter?"

"Surely you remember," Sara returned with saccharine sweetness. "The one from the *Rapid City Journal* who kept clinging to you as if she was afraid she might blow away. The brunette with the leather miniskirt and the big—"

He held up his hand, cutting her off. "I seem to vaguely remember someone fitting that description."

"'Why, Dr. Wilde, whatever is a handsome, intelligent man like you doing running away to join the circus?'" she mimicked the woman's sugary tone with a cold, precise perfection that would have made him smile had it not been for the building fury in her eyes.

"'Goodness, but this is such a horribly noisy place to conduct an interview; perhaps we can go somewhere a bit more quiet, more private.'" She batted her lashes in a biting parody of the eager young reporter. "'My apartment is only a few blocks away.'"

"I hadn't realized you included eavesdropping in your many attributes," he said easily.

"I wasn't eavesdroping. I just happened to overhear the conversation while I was walking past the van."

"Then you also heard me politely decline."

Sara met his even gaze with a furious one of her own. "Yes. But you certainly took your own sweet time about it," she snapped as she began digging furiously through her shoulder bag.

Darius decided that he liked it when her temper flared. An angry woman was not an indifferent one. When she muttered a particularly pungent oath, he couldn't resist a slight smile. Other women, when angry, might reach for a cigarette. Take a drink. Throw something. Sara, on the other hand, would search out chocolate.

"Here," he offered, taking a package of M&M chocolate peanuts out of his pocket and handing it to her.

"This doesn't change the fact that I was furious at you," she warned.

"If I was going to bribe you, Sara, I'd come up with something better than chocolate-covered peanuts. And for your information, I fully understand your feelings."

She looked up at him suspiciously. "You do?"

"I was ready to drop an Indian club on the head of that television reporter in Dayton."

"What reporter?"

"The one who trailed after you all day like a lovesick cocker spaniel."

"Oh, that one." Sara smiled. "He was cute, wasn't he?"

"He was okay, I guess. If you're into yuppies," Darius muttered.

Sara decided that she rather liked Darius's unexpected show of jealousy. In fact, she liked it a lot. "Personally, I prefer penguin-dancing anthropologists who have a habit of keeping chocolate in their pockets," she assured him as she popped one of the peanuts into her mouth. "Mmm. I'll say this for you, Darius, your taste in gifts is absolutely delicious."

"They should have been sapphires," he said, suddenly serious. "To match your eyes. They are incredible."

Sara stared up at him, momentarily unnerved by the intensity of his gaze. "Don't be silly," she said, struggling to keep the mood light, "chocolate-covered sapphires are definitely déclassé."

Darius watched with building frustration as she retreated behind the now all-too-familiar emotional barricades. He understood that she'd been hurt, accepted her need for caution, but dammit, he thought blackly, when was she going to open her eyes and see that he loved her? And that what they had was special.

"You know," he drawled, forcing a casual tone to match hers, "my little problem with that reporter was all your fault."

"My fault?"

"I was merely attempting to be polite for your sake, Sara."

Her hand flew to her chest. "*My* sake? If it had been up to me, Darius Wilde, I'd have tossed her right out on her leather-clad—"

"I didn't want to be responsible for the circus getting anything less than scintillating reviews."

Her blue eyes narrowed suspiciously. "Is that the truth?"

"The truth, the whole truth and nothing but the truth."

"Do you really expect me to believe that you weren't even the slightest bit tempted to take her up on her less than subtle offer? She was a beautiful, sexy woman, Darius!"

Terrific! Sara lambasted herself. *Great idea, pointing out all the available women who can't take their greedy little eyes off him whenever we hit a new town. Why don't you just open up a traveling dating service for the man while you're at it?*

He took her hand, running his hands over her knuckles. Darius had never been a demonstrative person; he had certainly never been a man who touched easily. Since meeting Sara, however, he seemed to have difficulty keeping his hands off her.

"Was she?" he murmured, mentally chalking up yet another change she had made in his life. "I didn't notice."

"And you were honestly only thinking of me?"

He saw a flash of dread in her eyes and realized that, for Sara, this was no joking matter. "I always think only of you, Sara. Every day. All day. Every night."

In the distance Darius could hear the low, threatening rumble of thunder, but he knew it wasn't the coming storm that had made Sara suddenly so tense. He winked to break the anxious mood. "*Especially* at night," he added with a slow, wolfish grin.

She laughed, as she was supposed to. And as she looked up into his laughing face, Sara felt the tension drain out of her like air out of a child's bright red balloon.

"All right," she decided, tossing her hair back over her shoulder in a decisive gesture, "you're off the hook. But just remember one thing."

He wrapped his arms around her waist and drew her to him. "What's that?"

"If I ever catch you accommodating one of those barracudas of the press, I'll feed you to the lions."

"The Peter and Wendy Family Circus and Penguin Extravaganza doesn't have any lions. Nor any tigers or bears, for that matter." His mouth brushed against Sara's temple, causing a jolt of exquisite lightning to run up her spine. "In fact, I seem to remember you explaining that putting innocent animals into cages and dragging them across the country was cruel and inhumane."

"Damn. You're right." She tilted her head back. "Then I'll just have to come up with something even more drastic," she warned.

"Why don't I simply promise not to stray?" He placed a light kiss on the bridge of her nose.

"Ah, but can I trust you? That's the sixty-four-thousand-dollar question."

"Of course. But just in case you're still harboring doubts as to my monogamous habits, sweetheart, perhaps you should keep me close by." He idly twined a lock of red-gold hair around his finger. "Somewhere you can keep an eye on me."

His good humor proved irresistibly contagious. No longer dwelling on imagined transgressions, Sara was only looking forward to the next few hours. Going up on her toes, she linked her arms around his neck. "Like my bed?"

"I always knew you were an intelligent woman, Sara McBride."

They laughed as their mouths met.

DAMASK—yards and yards of it—was adorned with ornately patterned trays fashioned of gleaming silver. Crystal—thin, long-stemmed glasses by Baccarat—captured the light from the chandelier overhead and split it into a thousand shimmering rainbows. The rich, heady scent of blue and white hothouse blooms blended enticingly with an amazing variety of perfumes and colognes.

The draped table groaned with food: small white pots of black caviar were accompanied by triangles of crisp golden toast and narrow wedges of lemon. There were Black Forest mushrooms sautéed in sweet butter, thin-skinned, deep purple Marseilles figs, thin slices of pink smoked salmon. Slices of rosy meat sprigged with dark green watercress rested on blue-and-white Royal Copenhagen porcelain. And delicate ices—lemon, boysenberry, raspberry—shimmered beside juicy Anjou pears.

Germaine Wingate was feeling pleased with herself, even a little smug, this evening. The caterer, bless his expensive little heart, had outdone himself. The musicians had arrived on time: the string quartet was ensconced in the garden, an absolutely gorgeous man—surely there must be someone she could fix him up with, Germaine mused—was strumming a Spanish guitar by the pool, and inside the stunning, mirrored salon a lovely harpist with romantic waist-length black hair—married, dammit—was beguiling her audience with her repertoire of Irish folk ballads.

Germaine had always been of the belief that the best way to ensure a successful party was to take a vastly dissimilar group of people, toss them together with more than enough food and drink, then sit back and watch them entertain themselves. Accordingly, her guest list was an intriguing potpourri of academia, business, the professions and the theater, with an occasional politician thrown in to keep things interesting. No one could remember a party of Germaine Wingate's failing, and tonight was proving no exception.

But her skill as a hostess was not what was bringing Germaine so much pleasure. Nor was it the fact that so many of her friends had shown up to celebrate her sixty-fifth birthday. Oh, that was rather sweet, she considered now, but not nearly as stimulating as the picture Darius and Sara made together.

Sara was presently engrossed in conversation with a tall, distinguished man Germaine knew to be the president of a major television network. Clad in an off-the-shoulder gown of floating silk in shades ranging from purely pink to scintillating scarlet, Sara brought to mind a wealthy gypsy. Gold hoops dangled from her ears; a trio of wide, hammered antique-gold bracelets encircled her slender arms. Her flaming hair tumbled down her back, inviting a man's fingers to play in the artfully tousled waves.

As Sara tossed her fiery head and laughed at something, Germaine decided that she'd never seen the young woman looking more beautiful. And from the shell-shocked expression on the network president's face, she knew she wasn't alone in her appraisal. Sara was not only lovely, but she exuded more fire and light than the aurora borealis. And if the tall, dark-haired man hovering by Sara's right elbow was not responsible for her condition, Germaine would hand in her matchmaker's card for good.

"She's a firecracker, that one," a deep voice beside her offered.

"Pure TNT," she agreed, turning to smile up at Judge Walter Cornell. "Good evening, Walter. I'm so pleased you were able to make it tonight."

Sara's paternal uncle was a tall, slender man with a shock of silver hair that topped a complexion deeply tanned from forty years of Sundays spent sculling on the Schuylkill River. He smiled as he lifted Germaine's outstretched hand to his lips.

"You should know that I'd never turn down an invitation from you, Germaine." His blue eyes twinkled. "I see my small token of esteem arrived in time."

Germaine lifted her hands to the emeralds twinkling at her ears. "Yes. And although I succumbed to temptation and wore them tonight because they matched my gown, the first thing tomorrow morning I'm having them returned to you by bonded courier."

He lifted a silver brow. "But why?"

"Because they are much too expensive, of course. People will talk."

"And what will they say?"

Germaine felt her skin grow warm. How many years had it been since she'd blushed? she wondered. "They'll say that we're lovers, of course."

He ran the back of his hand slowly down her powdered cheek. "If we're not, it isn't for lack of trying on my part."

She found herself held captive by the all-too-familiar warmth in his intimate gaze. This was ridiculous. She, a Frenchwoman known for her poise, was behaving like a foolish, tongue-tied schoolgirl. "Have you met Sara's beau?" she asked, desperate to change the subject.

Walter Cornell chuckled. "One of these days you're going to stop running, Germaine."

She could feel the curious gazes of a nearby circle of guests. "Really, Walter..."

He sighed. "All right, dear, I'll drop the subject for now. But don't take too long to change your mind; although age seems to have passed you by, I'm not getting any younger."

Walter Cornell had been her husband's best friend and the first person Germaine had met when Philip Wingate had returned home to his native Philadelphia. To her immense relief, she and Walter had hit it off immediately and had remained close friends even after Walter had married.

Now widowed for the past eighteen months, Walter had been lobbying for an even closer relationship and proposing on a regular basis. Germaine found the idea of marriage to the bold, outspoken jurist undeniably exciting and frightening at the same time. Valuing his friendship as she did, she was afraid to risk losing it if their love affair went wrong.

"You're not a minute older than when I first met you," she insisted with a soft, reminiscent smile. "Philip had raved about his best friend for months; I was terrified you wouldn't like me."

His answering smile matched hers, recalling shared memories. "And I was terrified my best friend would realize that I'd fallen head over heels in love with his new bride."

"Love?"

"If you'd been paying more heed to me, instead of lavishing attention on your husband, you would have realized how a man looks when he's been struck by lightning," Walter revealed.

Germaine's hand fluttered nervously to the neck of her green satin gown. "I never knew."

"I didn't want you to," he said simply. "There were too many people who could have been hurt if you ever felt tempted to return my feelings." He decided that it was some consolation, after forty years of keeping his silence, that the unflappable Germaine Wingate appeared to be tottering dangerously between disbelief and desire.

As if the shock waves generated by his confession were spreading outward, Sara suddenly turned away from her conversation and caught sight of Germaine's strangely distressed expression. Moments later she was working her way across the room, stopping to exchange greetings whenever necessary. Darius never left her side.

"Germaine, it's a marvelous party," she exclaimed, kissing the older woman on both cheeks. "But of course you know that."

"*Oui*," Germaine murmured distractedly.

Puzzled by Germaine's atypical behavior, Sara turned toward her uncle. "Uncle Walter," she greeted him with an enormous hug, "you are much too handsome to be running around unattached; I should talk to Germaine about putting her matchmaking talents to work on you."

"I've already inquired as to that possibility," Walter murmured.

Sara was suddenly aware of the undercurrents surrounding them. She stared up at Germaine, intrigued
by the soft flush on her friend's high, slanted cheekbones. Before she could comment, the older woman
had placed a slender hand on her arm.

"Sara, dear," she said, "I thought you should know
that Claire Taylor is here this evening."

A slight frown creased Sara's brow. "Claire?" The last
time she had seen Jeremy's former colleague had been
when the seemingly smug woman had arrived at the
apartment to retrieve his belongings.

Darius watched the silent exchange between the two
women: Germaine strangely apologetic, Sara obviously surprised, but struggling to conceal it. "How
nice," Sara managed. "I'll try to make a point of saying
hello."

Determined not to allow unhappy memories to ruin
what had thus far been a perfect evening, Sara turned
her attention back to her hostess. "You look absolutely
stunning, Germaine," she said. "And those earrings are
scrumptious. I don't believe I've ever seen them before.
Are they new?"

"*Oui*," the older woman said, her color rising even
more at the mention of the emerald jewelry. "You look
exquisite, *chérie*."

"Good. Because I feel absolutely exquisite." She
beamed up at Darius. "Don't I?"

Unable to resist, he ran his hand down her back.
"Absolutely exquisite," he agreed. "Germaine, *bon an-
niversaire*." He took her hand and lifted it to his lips

with a smooth, easy grace the average man would have had to have spent a lifetime perfecting.

"*Merci*, Darius, darling. My, you do know how to tempt a woman." She framed his smiling dark face in her hands. "If it were not for the fact that Sara is my godchild, I would whisk you right away—tonight—to the Riviera."

"If it weren't for the fact that Sara would feed me to the lions, I'd go."

"What makes you think I care two hoots about where you go? Or with whom?" Sara challenged.

Darius grinned. "You'll have to excuse Sara," he apologized. "She tends to get a little crabby when she's hungry. Something about low blood sugar."

"I beg your pardon?" Sara inquired frostily.

"You don't have to do that, sweetheart," he assured her, running his finger down the slope of her nose. "I certainly understand how a person can get out of sorts when they don't keep their strength up." He shook hands with Walter. "Judge Cornell, it's a pleasure seeing you again."

"The pleasure is all mine, Darius. It's refreshing to find my favorite niece in the company of a man who is almost good enough for her."

Sara, seething over Darius's uncomplimentary description, missed her uncle's openly appraising gaze. No one, for as far back as she could remember, had ever dared to call her crabby. Even her mother and father, who would never rank at the top of the Sara Cornell McBride fan club, were forced to admit that their daughter was irrepressibly personable. She tilted her chin.

"I am not crabby."

The gypsy had been momentarily replaced by an ice princess. Darius could practically see the jeweled tiara perched atop her flaming hair. The two personalities were as different as night and day. Darius adored both of them.

When he patted her on the head, Sara fumed. "Of course you are, sweetheart. And if you'll recall, I warned you that you should have eaten lunch," he reminded her with a bold, encouraging smile.

"If *I* remember correctly," Sara returned, "it was you who had other plans for lunchtime."

"Now, Sara," he chided mildly, "I'm sure neither Germaine nor your uncle are interested in our little secrets." He smiled at the avidly interested couple. "If you'll excuse me, I'll just get her a little bite to eat before she disturbs the other guests."

"Of course," Germaine agreed. It was a struggle to keep the smug smile from her face. "However, I'm certain Sara would never disturb anyone, Darius. She's always been such a delightful guest."

"And a delightful niece, as well," Walter offered. "Except for that one Christmas in England when she was seven and wandered off during a tour of the Midlands."

"I was looking for Little Nell's grave. And would the three of you kindly stop talking about me as if I weren't in the room?" Sara complained.

Darius took her hand. "Come along, dear, I'll fix you a plate."

Short of digging her heels into the black marble floor like a disobedient German Shepherd, Sara had no choice but to go along with him. For now.

"You just wait, Darius Wilde; you are definitely going to get yours," she threatened as he propelled her past the buffet table and through the French doors at the other end of the room.

"I was certainly planning on that," he agreed cheerfully. "Do you realize that it's been hours since we've made love?"

When they reached the garden, Sara breathed in the scent of newly mown grass and roses. "I'm furious at you."

He smiled down at her. "And well you should be. I acted outrageously, embarrassing you in front of Germaine and your uncle, dragging you out of the party in order to satisfy my own selfish needs to hold you. Kiss you."

Sara let out an annoyed breath. "Dammit, Darius—"

He toyed with one of the gold hoops in her ears. "What do you say we discuss this later?"

"We'll discuss it now," she insisted, even as he drew her closer with only the gentle touch of his fingers on her defiant chin.

"Sorry," he answered with a slow, patient smile, "but you seem to have your priorities confused, Sara. Right now I'm going to kiss you."

His hands were gentle as they settled on her silk-clad hips, but his body, as it pressed against hers, was strong, and hard, and undeniably arousing. It had grown dark, but the night was still warm. Sara could hear the sad sound of violins drifting on the sultry, scented air.

Then his lips claimed hers and the only sound she could hear was the blood humming in her veins.

"Wait here; I'll get you something to eat," he said after he released her a blissfully long time later.

Despite the clouds still fogging her mind, Sara decided that principle required that she at least lodge a formal protest. "Really, Darius, we should be going inside."

He touched his lips to hers, briefly, intimately. "I want you all to myself for just a little while," he said, running his hand down her bare arm. "Then, although I won't like it, I suppose I'll agree to share you."

"Golly, that's downright reasonable of you."

"Does that mean you'll wait here for me to get back?"

Sara decided that to insist otherwise, when she would honestly appreciate some time alone with Darius in the garden, would be cutting off her nose to spite her face. "Just don't take long," she instructed imperiously. "I'm suddenly starving."

He grinned. "I told you that you should have eaten lunch."

"I seem to remember you saying something about needing a nap before the party."

"I did. Was it my fault that the sex-crazed lady sharing my bed wouldn't let me sleep?" He practically oozed with self-satisfaction as he skimmed his hand down her cheek, then turned and disappeared into the crowd of people surrounding the pool.

Immersed in their sensual feelings for each other, Darius and Sara failed to notice the tall brunette woman who had been watching them intently from the shadows.

11

"HELLO, SARA. How nice to see that you've recovered so well from your unfortunate divorce," the woman said after Darius had disappeared inside the house.

Sara spun around as the all-too-familiar face emerged from the shadows. "Claire," she greeted her former husband's friend and colleague with a decided lack of enthusiasm. "This is a surprise; I hadn't realized you knew Germaine."

Slender shoulders clad in unrelieved black silk lifted and dropped in a careless shrug. "I don't, really. Actually, I'm here with a friend. Perhaps you know him. Matthew Downing?"

Sara did some rapid mental arithmetic. A well-known Philadelphia cardiologist, Matthew Downing was of the same generation as her uncle. That would make him more than twice Claire Taylor's age. "We've met. He's a nice man."

"Isn't he?" Claire agreed. "And recently widowed, poor thing." Her brown eyes gleamed in the muted glow of the landscape lighting.

Sara folded her arms over the brilliant bodice of her dress. "That's funny, I don't remember you being so interested in money."

"Everyone changes, Sara. You, me..." When she patted the intricate brown-black twist at the back of her neck, Sara caught the icy glimmer of diamonds on the ring finger of the woman's right hand. "Jeremy."

Claire paused just long enough to allow the name to linger on the perfumed night air. "Oh, my, you'd be amazed at exactly how much your former spouse has changed."

As much as she tried to avoid reacting to the sudden inclusion of Jeremy into this less than satisfactory conversation, Sara knew the other woman could hear her sudden intake of breath.

"You must have been to England recently," she managed to say through lips that had gone horribly dry.

Sara no longer loved Jeremy; she hadn't for years. So why did the mere mention of his name cause such a shock of pain to shoot through her? Because, she answered her own unspoken question, it invited too many comparisons between her ill-fated marriage and her current relationship with Darius. It also reminded her of personal failures she thought she had overcome.

"You didn't know?"

Sara knew she had just made Claire Taylor's evening. The sleek, sophisticated professor of medieval literature had always enjoyed putting Sara down in her own inimitable, cool fashion. It was beginning to feel like old times.

"All right, Claire," she said on an exasperated sigh. "I'll bite. What is it that you're obviously dying to tell me about Jeremy?"

"He's not living in England any longer."

"Good for him; he always complained that the damp climate gave him a perpetual cold."

"He's here."

"In Philadelphia?"

"No, silly. America. He's living in California."

Of all the places in the world that Sara might have guessed that her former husband had chosen to live, never in a million years would California have made the list. His derisive lecture on the decadence of the sun-bleached Pacific Coast state could go on for hours.

"California?" she echoed.

Claire nodded. "Malibu."

That was even more incredible. "I don't believe it."

The woman shot her an offended look. "Well, it's true. Matty and I were out there just last week and ran into him at Spago. He's writing for a television program," she announced.

If there was one thing Jeremy McBride had always hated worse than California—or circuses for that matter—it was television. He had always considered it nothing but pap, to the point of not allowing a set in their apartment. In fact, Sara realized now, the only program her former husband had occasionally deigned to watch was *Masterpiece Theater*, which he would view at the faculty lounge at the university, then spend the next week complaining that classic British literature was being debased by television.

"I can't picture Jeremy writing for television," Sara admitted after a long pause.

"Oh, he isn't working on anything trite. Goodness, the man's far too talented to waste his skills writing situation comedies or those horrid police shows."

Sara wasn't particularly surprised to discover that she had not the slightest interest in Jeremy's current project. "Well, I certainly hope he's happy," she said, trying to sound as if she meant it. "It's been nice chatting with you, Claire, but I really have to go in now. I'm on the verge of starving to death." She turned abruptly, almost walking straight into Darius as she left the garden.

"Who was that?" he asked, handing her a plate piled high with food.

"Merely the Ghost of Christmas Past," she murmured, sinking down into a chair at a nearby glass-topped table. The unexpected exchange had left her strangely shaky.

"You didn't look particularly thrilled to see her," Darius probed gently. He had observed the brief conversation between the women from the edge of the flagstone terrace. Although Sara had kept a bland, polite smile on her lips, it had been obvious that she was tense and more than a little discomfited by the encounter.

Sara took a sip of champagne before answering. It was cool and brisk on her tongue. "She was a colleague of Jeremy's at the university."

Something in her muted tone caught his immediate attention. "Was that all?"

She shrugged, wishing they hadn't gotten onto the unpalatable subject in the first place. "I don't know; I think so. I can't really imagine Jeremy having an affair. Not when he was always so enamored of himself."

Darius ran his hand down her hair in a gesture that was meant to soothe rather than arouse. "The guy really did a number on you, didn't he?"

If anyone had suggested such a thing fourteen short weeks ago, Sara would have insisted that they were wrong. For six months after her child's death, she had behaved like a zombie, uninterested in everyone and everything around her. Finally, with the help of her family, and her friends—like Germaine, Helga, Yuri and the other members of the troupe—she had managed to survive.

One way she'd done that had been by throwing herself into her work, turning the NewMarket Players into the now critically acclaimed Peter and Wendy Family Circus and Penguin Extravaganza. The group of performers were in constant demand, their touring season expanding from four weeks that first year to sixteen weeks. During the remainder of the year they performed before standing-room-only crowds at the Zellerback Theater and the historic Walnut Street Theater, among others.

Sara had assured herself that she was satisfied with her life. Even happy. But Claire's unexpected appearance, and her reaction to it, forced her to consider the fact that perhaps the injuries inflicted by the breakup of her marriage had gone deeper than she'd led herself to believe.

"I don't want to talk about him anymore," she insisted, jumping to her feet. Her appetite had suddenly vanished. "Come back inside with me, Darius. We've never danced together and I've just realized that it's been absolutely ages since I waltzed." Linking their fingers, she practically dragged him back into the house.

Making their way through the throng of partygoers, they had nearly reached the dance floor when Sara groaned softly under her breath.

"What's wrong?" Darius asked.

"My parents." She exhaled a soft, rippling sigh of acceptance. "Well, since we're not going to avoid talking with them, keep your fingers crossed. With any luck we can escape before my father gets around to asking you your intentions."

Personally, Darius would have enjoyed an opportunity to tell someone other than Yuri his feelings concerning Sara. Although in the past he'd preferred to keep his personal feelings close to the vest, lately he'd been having the almost overwhelming urge to shout his love from the highest rooftops.

Her parents could have stepped off the glossy pages of *Town and Country* magazine. Her father, Andrew Cornell, was remarkably handsome—tall, lean and darkly tanned. Dressed in a custom-tailored dinner jacket, he radiated an aura of overwhelming self-confidence. Standing beside him in a white floor-length silk sheath, icy diamonds sparkling at her ears and neck, Julia Cornell's delicate, aristocratic features were a perfect foil to her husband's robust good looks.

Darius would have recognized Sara's mother anywhere. Although her hair had been fashioned into a sleek, intricate twist at the back of her neck, it had the same red-gold sheen as her daughter's. Julia's eyes—like Sara's—were wide, dominating the exquisite bone structure of her face. But, unlike Sara's dancing blue eyes, her mother's brought to mind an arctic glacier. As they flicked speculatively over Darius, he almost imagined he could feel the chill.

"Hello, Mother," Sara greeted the older woman. She was, Darius noted, uncharacteristically subdued. "You look lovely. As always."

Julia's answering smile was as cold and remote as her eyes. "Why, thank you, dear. And don't you look nice? That dress is such a pleasant change from your usual casual attire. Although I'd never in a million years have the nerve to wear that color, on you, somehow, it seems to work."

She turned her attention to Darius. "Are you going to remember your manners and introduce us to your young man, Sara?"

Sara's answering tone was flat, entirely devoid of expression. "Mother, Father, I'd like you to meet Dr. Darius Wilde. Darius, these are my parents."

Unable to shake hands, since Sara's fingers were still tightly entwined with his, Darius simply nodded. "How do you do, Mrs. Cornell. Mr. Cornell," he answered politely. "May I offer a belated congratulations on your recent anniversary."

"Why, thank you, Dr. Wilde," Julia said. "However did you know about that?"

"Sara showed me the seascape she'd painted for you," Darius explained conversationally. "You must have been extremely moved that she managed to take precious time from her busy schedule in order to complete it in time for the festive occasion."

For a moment Julia appeared speechless. She recovered quickly. "Yes. Of course we were extremely moved."

Darius smiled approvingly. "Of course you were. I hope you realize that you're very lucky."

Julia arched a perfectly shaped brow. "Lucky?"

"To have a Sara McBride original gracing your bedroom wall; I've been trying for weeks to talk Sara into painting a similar one for me."

"Really?"

"That's right. I even suggested that if you and your husband didn't want yours, Sara might consider giving it to me instead. But of course the very idea that a woman such as you wouldn't have the extreme good taste to appreciate such an energetic artistic effort was ridiculous. Wasn't it?"

"Ridiculous," Julia echoed weakly.

He nodded. "Of course. So I suppose for the time being I'll just have to forgo the pleasure of having one of Sara's paintings hanging on my wall."

Point made, he turned his attention to her father. "You know your daughter, sir, always on the go. I've been rightfully accused of being a workaholic, but Sara puts me to shame. She's amazing; but of course I don't have to tell you that."

Andrew Cornell appeared nearly as discomfited as his wife by Darius's words of praise for his daughter. "Sara always did have a great deal of energy," he agreed dismissingly. "Although from what I've read about your work, I have a hard time believing that anyone could put you to shame. Needless to say, Dr. Wilde, Mrs. Cornell and I were quite surprised when Germaine told us about your proposed project."

"My husband and I have read all your books; your work sounds absolutely fascinating, Dr. Wilde," Julia broke in.

"Which makes us wonder, naturally, why you're spending this summer with our daughter," Andrew added.

When Sara's fingers abruptly turned cold in his, Darius bit back a sharp response. If he were to lose his rapidly escalating temper, he would only succeed in embarrassing Sara and casting a pall over Germaine's birthday celebration. He cared too much about both women to risk doing that.

"What do you mean?" he asked in a deceptively calm tone.

"As an anthropologist, you've always dealt with serious, important issues," Andrew pointed out unnecessarily. "Surely you can't profess that chronicling the daily activities of a small, itinerant circus—" he heaped an extra helping of scorn on the word "—begins to measure up to your previous work."

As Darius's eyes met Sara's, he allowed all of his love to show in his steady dark gaze. "Believe me, Mr. Cornell," he stated gravely, "I take this current project more seriously than I've ever taken anything in my life."

As Sara stared up at the unmasked emotion swirling across his face, she felt as if the world had suddenly stopped spinning. Just when she was certain that she was never going to breathe again, Darius grinned and the overwhelmingly intimate moment had passed.

"Now if you'll excuse me, Mrs. Cornell, Mr. Cornell," he said with extreme politeness, "your daughter's been begging me to dance with her. And you know how difficult it is to deny Sara anything." With a brief dismissing nod he led her out onto the dance floor.

"Thank you," Sara murmured.

"You're welcome. For what?"

"Sticking up for the circus. And for me."

Darius shrugged. "Hey, that was the easy part. The difficult part was not calling your father a short-sighted, intellectual snob. And telling that frigid iceberg posing as a mother that you've got more class in your little finger than she'll ever have in her whole body."

Sara smiled. "You really are good for me, you know."

Darius lifted her hand to his lips. "I know. And you're good for me. How about we get out of here and discuss exactly how good we can be together?"

As his lips brushed her knuckles, Sara could feel the heat rise. "You promised me a dance," she reminded him.

"At least this way I get to hold you," he said fatalistically as he took her into his arms. "Well, here goes. How do you know I won't step on your toes?"

When she tilted her head back to look up at him, Darius was relieved to see that her eyes had regained some of their impish sparkle. "Any man who can dance the penguin extravaganza finale can undoubtedly waltz without crushing toes," she decided.

"Speaking of that," he murmured, drawing her closer, "you are, of course, aware that Orrin's been back on his feet for more than a week."

Forgoing the proper dancing school posture that she had unwillingly learned at Madame Fontaine's when she was twelve, Sara rested her cheek on his shoulder. "I know. We were so lucky that he wasn't seriously injured."

"Lucky." His lips brushed her hair. "So when do I get relieved from the penguin chorus line?"

"Oh, thirteen penguins make a much better extravaganza than twelve."

"I thought Helga had choreographed the dance for an even dozen. Remember, that's why I was drafted in the first place."

"She changed it." Sara gave him a warm, enticing smile. "It's only for two more weeks, Darius."

Darius wondered if their daughters would inherit those wide blue eyes and darkly pink lips. If they did, in order to avoid raising a family of spoiled brats, he supposed that Sara would have to take on the job of disciplinarian. Time after time over the past fourteen weeks, he had proved himself unable to resist their seductive appeal.

"Two weeks," he agreed. "Then I'm retiring the penguin suit. For good. And next time I'm not going to allow you to change my mind."

"I wouldn't think of it," she agreed immediately. Her innocent tone didn't fool him in the least. Darius had the feeling that this would not be the last summer he'd be conned, coaxed or beguiled into performing in her precious penguin extravaganza.

"By the way," she said, "my parents still haven't taken their eyes off us. Since I haven't managed to scandalize them yet this evening, how would you feel about helping their black-sheep daughter live up to her reputation?"

His mouth twitched in a smile. "I could probably go along with that." His fingers tightened on her waist. The silk was soft under his touch; Darius knew that her skin was softer still. "Got any ideas?"

"I was hoping you'd have some."

He pretended to consider the matter as they swayed slowly to the music. He could feel his body coming alive and struggled to regain control. If he wasn't careful, he actually *would* end up embarrassing them both. Not to mention her parents. Germaine, he knew, would only be amused that Sara had the power to bewitch his traitorous body into betraying him with only the slightest provocation.

"What would you say to me throwing you down onto the dance floor and having my way with you?" he suggested. "Right here and now."

His touch was searing the thin material to her skin. Her pulse began beating faster. Then faster still. "That's probably a bit excessive," she said with a regretful little sigh. "Even for a black sheep like me."

"I was afraid you'd say that." His fingers brushed tantalizingly up and down the curve where her slender waist flared into sensuous hips. "How about I just kiss you, then? For now."

"For now." Her gaze, as it locked with his, promised hot, intimate secrets. Then, framing his face in her palms, Sara urged his mouth down to hers.

THE MOON WAS FULL and white, filling the loft with an otherworldly glow as Darius and Sara lay side by side and allowed the world to slowly settle. The woven rug under their bodies offered scant padding, but just as they'd both been too impatient upon returning to Darius's loft to make their way to his wide bed, now they were too warmly complacent to move. Darius's arms were wrapped around Sara; her hair was splayed over his chest like tongues of flame.

In the background music was playing. Oscar Peterson's piano had given way to Miles Davis's trumpet, which in turn had given way to Billie Holiday. The lights were low, the room filled with deep purple shadows that were somehow suited to the slow, sultry notes.

As she trailed her fingers idly through his dark chest hair, Sara remembered the warm taste of Darius's mouth. Her renewed arousal, so soon after making love, was every bit as sharp as it was sweet.

"I've always liked Billie Holiday," she murmured, growing breathless as his fingers whispered over her breasts. Would it always be like this? Sara wondered. Would he only have to touch her, look at her, to have her wanting him? Needing him? The idea that anyone, even Darius, should have such power over her was less appealing. It made her all too vulnerable for her own good.

"Me, too. But not as much as I like you. Have I mentioned that you're the most beautiful woman I've ever seen?" He punctuated his words with light, feathery kisses. "And that even now, after all we've shared, after just having made love, I want you more than any woman I've ever known?"

"I want you, too," she whispered.

"You don't sound very happy about that." He tilted his head back and looked down into her face for a long, thoughtful time. "I love you, Sara."

She stiffened in his arms. "You don't have to say that. I'm not like other women, Darius. I don't need the words."

She was trembling once again, but Darius knew it was from fear, not passion. He drew her to him. "Perhaps not. But I've suddenly found that I do."

He took a deep breath, wondering where to begin. "My father always swore that he fell in love with my mother at first sight. As much as I respected him— loved him—I could never quite accept that idea." His gaze swept her distressed face. "Until now. Until you."

"Darius, really, you don't have to—"

He pressed his fingers against her lips. "Yes," he insisted quietly. Firmly. "I do. I want you to understand that I take these things very seriously, Sara. My father has had one true love—my mother. I've watched them all my life, laughing together, fighting together, but always loving together. And I swore that I was never going to accept anything less for myself."

"No." She pulled away from him, reaching around frantically on the floor for her scattered clothing. "I don't want to hear this; it doesn't have anything to do with who we are. What we have together."

How could she be so open with her emotions, yet still be able to close her eyes to the love that had sprung up, full-blown, between them, Darius wondered. He realized belatedly that his timing was definitely off. All too often, Sara's saucy bohemian brilliance caused him to forget how vulnerable she really was.

He'd kept his mouth shut this long; he should have waited two more weeks until the end of the tour before announcing his intentions. But now that he'd blundered into it, he knew the only answer was to keep on going.

"Doesn't it?"

She tugged a pair of bikini panties over her hips. "Not at all," she lied unconvincingly.

A very strong part of Sara wanted nothing more than to accept Darius's love. Another more cautious part was afraid that in doing so she would only be setting herself up for additional heartache. She reached behind her back, struggling as she attempted to fasten her strapless bra with fingers that had gone strangely numb.

"We've been getting along so well," she complained. "Why do you have to ruin things?"

His temper flared at her uncomplimentary response to his declaration of love, but Darius controlled it. "I don't want to ruin things," he answered as she pulled the dress over her head, which momentarily disappeared beneath layers of scarlet silk. "I want to marry you."

She went ice-cold. Head, hands, feet. Her heart froze, then began pounding so loudly that Sara wondered if Darius could hear it. "No," she whispered.

Darius wanted to go to her, to take her in his arms and comfort her, but a lingering vestige of pride made him keep his distance. He'd only professed his love to one woman: Sara. He'd only, in all his thirty-three years, proposed to one woman: again, Sara. The words had not come easily; to have them thrown so carelessly back at him was distinctly frustrating. He forced himself to take a deep breath and begin again.

"Sweetheart," he murmured getting up from the floor and going over to stand in front of her. "I love you; you don't have to be afraid of me."

Sara backed away as he reached for her. How could he not understand? His love was precisely what she found so terrifying. If she allowed herself to love him back, which she was already afraid had happened, the next logical step would be marriage. She'd already proven herself to be a failure at marriage. And if there were children . . .

She pressed her hand against her heart, as if trying to prevent it from shattering into a million pieces. No, she wouldn't, couldn't allow herself to even consider the possibility of children. The agony of losing Amy had almost destroyed her; Sara couldn't risk that much pain again. Not even for Darius.

"We've been getting along so well," she complained again in a frail, ragged voice. "Why can't we keep things as they are?"

"Because I don't like things the way they are, dammit. I want to marry you, Sara. Live with you. Have children with you."

His words made Sara turn pale. She shook her head, turning away as her eyes filled with tears.

Damn. Darius regretted the incautious declaration the moment it had escaped his lips. He was a scholar. A writer. A man used to carefully weighing every word, every turn of phrase, seeking the most effective way to get his point across. Yet here he was, behaving like a raving idiot. If this is what love did to you, Darius considered blackly, he was glad he'd only had to suffer the consequences once in his lifetime.

"Sara, sweetheart." Ignoring her frantic, whispered protests, he drew her into his arms. "I can understand how painful your experience with Amy must have been. But it doesn't have to be that way again."

"I don't want to talk about Amy." Her hands pushed ineffectively at his chest.

Darius tightened his hold. "We have to. You have to understand that it doesn't have to happen again. There's been a lot of research on SIDS in the past few years; a friend of mine who's on the faculty of Pomona College in California is heading a project looking into possible causes. And there are precautions that can be taken."

"I said I don't want to talk about it," Sara insisted, her voice rising to an unnaturally high pitch. "And I want you to let me go, Darius. Now."

"All right." He dropped his hands to his sides, even though he wanted to continue holding her. "We're going to have to discuss it eventually, Sara," he warned in a low, dangerously quiet voice. "But until then, there's one thing you need to keep in mind."

Traitorous tears had begun to fall; Sara dashed them away with the back of her hand. "What's that?"

His eyes were like chips of obsidian. Hard and black as midnight. "I'm nothing like Jeremy McBride. I'm not going to wash my hands of you or our relationship simply because things have gotten a little rough."

A little rough? He was tearing her heart out piece by piece and he called it a little rough? Sara's eyes desperately searched the floor for her shoes. She had to leave. Now. While she still could.

"I love you," he said again, aching deep inside as his words made her flinch. "I'll always love you. And we're not finished yet, Sara. Not by a long shot."

Her eyes glazed with tears, Sara gave up on locating her shoes. "I can't handle this," she insisted shakily. "Not now. Not ever. Goodbye, Darius. I'm sorry."

She was out the door before he could make a move to stop her. Although he knew that he could easily catch her before she reached the street, Darius also understood that she needed some time alone to think things through. He watched from the window as she ran to her car and, with a desperate squeal of the tires, drove away, disappearing into the night.

He had always considered himself a patient man; his work had depended on that particular personality trait. Since meeting Sara McBride, however he had discovered exactly how impatient he could be. Darius knew that the coming days were going to prove the longest, not to mention most frustrating, of his life.

12

VENICE, CALIFORNIA, was a theater of the absurd. Although Mack Sennett's Bathing Beauties no longer cavorted on the Venice beach and the days of Sarah Bernhardt, Charlie Chaplin and Mary Pickford performing in the city of canals had faded into distant memory, the exotic beachfront town still maintained its share of entertainers.

Magicians, musicians and whitefaced mimes made the streets their stage while bicyclists and roller skaters—most of them wired for sound—rolled along the Ocean Front Walk.

Usually Sara found Venice a delight for the senses. This year, however, it seemed as if nothing could lift her spirits. All six final performances had been sold out weeks in advance. In addition to that success, they had been featured on a number of local television programs. One such appearance, on *Good Morning L.A.*, had even been picked up by the network, garnering the Peter and Wendy Family Circus and Penguin Extravaganza national coverage.

At any other time Sara would have been thrilled by the publicity. But all she could think about was Darius. And their last time together.

She hadn't heard from him for fourteen very long and very lonely days. And as much as she wanted to assure herself that it was for the best, she was finding lying to herself even more difficult than lying to Darius.

She loved him. If she were to be honest with herself, Sara would probably have to admit that she had always loved him. From that first moment she'd looked up and seen him standing there, looking remarkably at ease in what could charitably be described as chaos. During their time together she had come to realize exactly what had made him such a success at his work: Darius Wilde had the uncanny ability to fit in anywhere, with anyone, while still maintaining his own unique personality.

Less than two short weeks ago, Sara had still been trying to convince herself that living with Darius would be impossible; now she knew that the impossibility would be to continue living without him.

"Go to him," Helga insisted for the umpteenth time. "Your pride is not worth the cost of your heart. Believe me."

Sara smeared thick white cold cream over her face. "That's easy for you to say," she murmured. "You're already married."

"*Ja,*" Helga agreed. "And I've already told you that it was I who went to him."

"That was different," Sara argued as she began wiping the cold cream off with a handful of tissues. "Yuri obviously adores you."

"And Darius adores you. So what is the problem?"

"The problem?" Sara's eyes, as they met her friend's in the mirror, were absolutely bleak. "What if he's changed his mind? What if he doesn't want me any longer?"

"Then you'll carry on," Helga said with her indefatigable practicality. "As you have before." Her reflected expression was openly sympathetic. "Life doesn't come with guarantees, Sara. But I still believe that your Darius Wilde is the closest you'll ever get to a sure thing."

She rose from the chair in a smooth, graceful movement and crossed the room to give Sara a brief, reassuring hug. "He's a good man, Sara. Everything will work out. Believe me."

Sara managed a wobbly smile of her own. "You've no idea how much I hope that you're right."

"I always am," Helga responded smoothly. "Go to him, Sara. You won't regret it," she insisted. With that she was gone.

By the time Sara had removed the last of her makeup, she had made a decision. Fifteen minutes later she was packing her clothes. Deep in thought, she failed to hear Darius enter the tent.

"Hello, Sara." At the sound of his familiar voice, her heart stopped. Then lurched. Then began beating again. Taking a deep breath that should have calmed but didn't, she slowly turned around.

"You're back." Her voice was reasonably steady, considering the circumstances, but her face revealed her relief.

"I told you that I wasn't going to give up," Darius reminded her quietly.

"I've missed you." She was too pale, and there were dark circles under her eyes. But as Sara stared up at him, all her love shining in those soft blue eyes, he couldn't remember ever seeing her look so lovely.

He crossed the small expanse between them. "Not as much as I've missed you," he murmured, lacing his hands through her hair.

He bent his head, kissing her heatedly, fiercely. Sara clung to him, her own need every bit as urgent. Yet as much as Darius wanted her now, there was something they had to settle first.

"You are going to marry me, aren't you?"

Sara tilted her head back, studying him carefully as her fingers smoothed at the tension lines etched on his dark features. "I won't be a traditional, professor's wife," she warned.

"Then we're even. Because I've never been a traditional professor." He began unbuttoning her yellow cotton blouse.

"I hate faculty teas and I've never had the patience to learn bridge."

"That's okay; I hate bridge and I've never enjoyed stuffy faculty teas, either. Although those little short-bread cookies aren't so bad," he said consideringly. The blouse fell unheeded to the floor, followed in short order by his white polo shirt.

"We can always buy those at the supermarket," she suggested breathlessly as his fingers moved to the zipper at her waist.

"My God, you are an intelligent woman." He tugged, and the skirt fell to the floor of the tent in a soft cloud of yellow gauze. "No wonder I fell in love with you."

Love. Was there any more entrancing word in the English language? Sara wondered. "Really?" she inquired, laughing, as she stepped out of the skirt. "And here I fell in love with you because I adore the way you look in your penguin suit."

That ridiculous outfit was not Darius's favorite topic of conversation. He'd agreed to wear it because he loved Sara. But that didn't mean he had to like it.

"You really know how to boost a guy's ego, don't you, sweetheart?"

"I certainly try," she agreed sweetly. "I'll still want to tour with the circus in the summer."

"Great. They say travel is broadening for children." As soon as he'd said the words, Darius regretted them. He held his breath, waiting for Sara to stiffen in his arms.

But she had already come to grips with her fears during these last lonely nights in California. Nights that had allowed a period of intense introspection. She knew that there were risks involved with loving Darius. With having his children. The difference was that this time she and Darius would be facing them together.

"That's what they say," she agreed breathlessly as her fingers toyed with his belt buckle.

Relief washed over him in cooling waves. Darius swept her up and carried her to the overstuffed armchair. Past experience had taught him that the narrow cot was impossible. "Next year we're bringing along a better bed," he muttered as he pulled her onto his lap. "Even if we have to add another truck to the caravan to carry it."

"Agreed."

"As for now, what are you doing for the rest of the evening?"

"Making love to you," Sara answered promptly, pulling his head down to hers.

"How about for the rest of your life?" he asked against her lips.

Sara tilted her head back and smiled up at him. "Making love to you."

Epilogue

SARA FROWNED as she turned this way and that, studying her reflection in the full-length bedroom mirror. No doubt about it, she was definitely gaining weight. This time next month people would be mistaking her for the Goodyear blimp.

"By the time we're halfway through this year's tour, I won't need any padding to play Sassy Sally," she complained.

Darius looked up from fastening the ebony studs on the starched white front of his shirt. "I think you look gorgeous," he said as his dark eyes took in her softly rounded figure, attractively draped in gleaming blue silk.

"You're prejudiced."

He grinned. "Of course. But that doesn't change the fact that you're lovely."

Sara sighed. "I can't understand it; I didn't put on nearly this much weight with Maddy."

"Maddy wasn't twins," he reminded her.

"No, she simply manages, in her own inimitable way, to cause every bit as many problems as two children," Sara commented dryly.

"She was wondering if you're going to kiss her goodnight before we leave for the party."

"Of course. I'd planned to go in after the sitter put her to bed. Why wouldn't I?"

"She's afraid you're still upset about Bogie."

Sara raised a russet brow. "Upset? Why should I be upset simply because my two-year-old daughter painted fluorescent orange stripes on her black kitten?"

"It wasn't her fault she had to improvise when it came to locating a tiger for her wild animal act," Darius interceded. "It really isn't all that different from the time you drafted McGregor into service, sweetheart."

Sara laughed, recalling the summer she had shaved the Cornell family collie, leaving only his thick neck ruff and a ragged tuft at the end of his tail. Like Maddy, she had been forced to improvise when it had come to finding a lion for the neighborhood circus she had organized.

"I never should have told you all my secrets," she complained. "All right, you win. As usual. Tell your delinquent daughter that I'll be in as soon as I finish dressing."

Darius caught her hand as she reached into her jewelry box, searching out the pearls that her uncle had given her on her wedding day. "Wait."

"We're already running late."

"Germaine and Walter will understand if we show up a few minutes late for their anniversary party. I have something for you."

A smile lit up her face. "Oh, good. I love presents."

"I know." He retrieved a small box with the unmistakable shape of a candy kiss package from the pocket of his dress slacks. "And I love giving them to you."

"Chocolate," she said happily. "However did you know that I've been dreaming of Hershey's kisses ever since I went on that stupid diet last week. And by the way, now that I know that there's a legitimate reason for this ridiculous weight gain, I'm going to give it up so I can enjoy myself at Germaine's tonight. She wouldn't tell me the menu ahead of time—she's such a stickler about wanting everything to be a surprise—but she always has such delicious . . ."

Sara's voice trailed off and her breath caught in her throat as she opened the box and saw the flawless sapphires lying on their bed of white satin.

"Like them?" Darius asked with undue casualness. He wondered if she could tell that he was holding his breath.

Sara lifted the earrings up to the light, reveling in their brilliance. The rich, deep color echoed the intense, swirling blues of the seascape hanging on their bedroom wall.

"I adore them; they're the most gorgeous things I've ever seen," she admitted breathlessly. "But can we afford them?"

"I received a royalty check for the Peter and Wendy book this morning; you'll be pleased to know that sales for *The Grand Charivari* just topped *Drumbeats*."

Sara was flushed with pleasure. For herself and her circus. But most of all for her husband.

"I'm so happy," she whispered as she looked up at him.

Viewing the uncensored love shining in her wide blue eyes—eyes that their daughter had inherited—Darius wondered how it was that Sara could grow more lovely with each passing day. Three years and he still couldn't believe his luck.

He took the earrings from her hand and slipped them into the holes in her earlobes, then turned her to face the mirror. The perfectly cut stones glittered like blue ice against the warmth of her skin.

"I knew it," he murmured as he nuzzled her neck.

"Knew what?" Sara asked softly, entranced by the sight of the flawless sapphires twinkling at her ears.

"That they'd match your eyes."

Blue eyes met gleaming ebony eyes in the mirror. Together they watched his hands skim over the cobalt silk, exploring the gently swelling curves of her body. Three children, Germaine had promised him during that long-ago lunch. And a wife. Once again it seemed that her crystal ball had been telling the truth. First there had been Sara. Then Maddy. And now twins. What had he ever done right in his life to deserve such happiness? he wondered.

"Exactly how late are we?" Darius questioned as the familiar heat sizzled. He had a sudden urge to see her naked, wearing only his gleaming sapphires in her ears.

Sara found herself fantasizing an identical scenario. With a low, sultry laugh she turned in his arms. "Not that late. Besides, it's fashionable to be late."

He grinned down at her. "Using that logic, Germaine would probably be the first to approve, since she's nothing if not fashionable."

"You are so incredibly sexy when you're being logical, Professor Wilde." Sara framed his face with her palms. "Let's be fashionable, Darius," she said with a slow, inviting smile that caused heat to run up his spine. "Let's be very, very fashionable together."

Harlequin Temptation

COMING NEXT MONTH

JOIN THE CELEBRATION!
THE FIFTH ANNIVERSARY
OF HARLEQUIN
AMERICAN ROMANCE

1988 is a banner year for Harlequin American Romance—it marks our fifth anniversary.

For five successful years we've been bringing you heartwarming, exciting romances, but we're not stopping there. In August, 1988, we've got an extraspecial treat for you. Join us next month when we feature four of American Romance's best—and four favorite—authors.

Judith Arnold, Rebecca Flanders, Beverly Sommers and Anne Stuart will enchant you with the stories of four women friends who lived in the same New York apartment building and whose lives, one by one, take an unexpected turn. Meet Abbie, Jaime, Suzanne and Marielle—the women of YORKTOWN TOWERS.

Four believable American Romance heroines…four contemporary American women just like you…by four of your favorite American Romance authors.

Don't miss these special stories. Enjoy the fifth-anniversary celebration of Harlequin American Romance!